SO MUCH FOR
DEMOCRACY

SO MUCH FOR DEMOCRACY

KARI JONES

ORCA BOOK PUBLISHERS

Library and Archives Canada Cataloguing in Publication

Jones, Kari, 1966-, author
So much for democracy / Kari Jones.

Issued in print and electronic formats.
ISBN 978-1-4598-0481-4 (pbk.).--ISBN 978-1-45980-760-0 (bound)
ISBN 978-1-4598-0482-1 (pdf).--ISBN 978-1-4598-0483-8 (epub)

I. Title.
PS8619.O5328S6 2014   jc813'.6   C2013-906650-0
                             C2013-906651-9

First published in the United States, 2014
Library of Congress Control Number: 2013954146

Summary: The political upheaval in Ghana in 1979
puts Astrid and the rest of her Canadian family at risk.

*Orca Book Publishers is dedicated to preserving the environment and
has printed this book on Forest Stewardship Council® certified paper.*

Orca Book Publishers gratefully acknowledges the support for its publishing programs
provided by the following agencies: the Government of Canada through the Canada Book
Fund and the Canada Council for the Arts, and the Province of British Columbia
through the BC Arts Council and the Book Publishing Tax Credit.

Cover design by Chantal Gabriell
Cover artwork by Janice Kun
Author photo courtesy of Camosun College

ORCA BOOK PUBLISHERS   ORCA BOOK PUBLISHERS
PO Box 5626, Stn. B   PO Box 468
Victoria, BC Canada   Custer, WA USA
v8R 6s4   98240-0468

www.orcabook.com
Printed and bound in Canada.

17 16 15 14 • 4 3 2 1

To Dawn and Terry and Bruce,
for the Ghana years.

ONE

"Astrid, are you listening to me?" asks Mom.

I nod, but I'm not, because she tells me exactly the same things every morning. *Don't talk to anyone you don't know, don't eat anything unless it's made in our kitchen, don't drink anything unless it's from a sealed bottle, don't touch anything and, most of all, don't go anywhere without asking.* Those are the rules.

"I know, Mom," I say as I pull my school uniform on over my head and check myself in the mirror. "I'm twelve. I can remember the rules."

She stands behind me and smooths the neck of my uniform until I twist away and say, "Mom, you'd better get Piper up or we'll be late for school."

She tucks a strand of hair behind my ear and says, "Go have some breakfast. We'll be right down."

I pull the hair out from behind my ear and adjust the neck of my uniform, then slip my feet into my sandals. I take one last look at myself in the mirror, inhale deeply and then exhale.

It's not easy living with my mom these days. She's getting so overprotective.

I'm not hungry, so I go outside to wait for Mom to drive us to school. My little brother, Gordo, and Thomas, the gardener, are already there, peering at something dangling from one of the hibiscus bushes. It's some kind of spider, possibly deadly.

"What is it?" I ask Thomas, since there's no point talking to Gordo when he's watching any kind of creature. Gordo's only ten, but he knows more about nature than most adults, and when he's focused on something he finds interesting, it's like he forgets anyone else is even there.

"It's a weaver," says Thomas.

"Is it poisonous?" I ask.

Thomas leans on his shovel and says, "Now Asteroid, do you think I'd let Gordo get that close to a poisonous spider?" Thomas smiles when he calls me Asteroid, which is a play on my name. I like that we share a private joke.

Thomas knows everything there is to know about our garden and the plants and animals in it. Most of them he points out to Gordo, but I did catch him once placing some cobra eggs in a bucket to take away before Gordo found them.

I shouldn't have worried about the spider being poisonous.

The wind rattles the hibiscus bushes, and sand blows into my eyes. Thomas calls this wind the Harmattan and says it comes all the way across West Africa from the Sahara. When he first told us that, I didn't know whether to believe him, since Accra's on the ocean and nowhere near the desert, but I looked it up in the encyclopedia, and he was right. Ever since we got here, three months ago in the middle of January, sand's been making our food crunchy and getting into our eyes. The rains are supposed to start soon, though, which will be a relief.

Thomas points to the spider and says, "Make sure to keep Piper away. It's not poisonous, but it still hurts if it bites."

"I will," I say.

Piper is two and has hair like a chick's down. In Accra, having white skin and blond hair is like wearing a sign that says *stare at me*. Even my own sandy-blond hair makes people gape. Strangers cluck at Piper when we walk down the street. Kids skip across lanes of traffic and try to stroke her cheek. I give them an ice-queen stare because Mom says we shouldn't let people we don't know touch her. But Piper smiles right at them, and they smile back.

When Mom comes out to take us to school, Gordo looks up and starts to tell her what he's found, but I interrupt him. "Thomas says the mangoes will be ripe soon."

I nudge Gordo as I speak, and he sighs but steps away from the bush. Thomas nods and smiles at Mom.

We're all getting good at hiding things from her.

Mom thinks there's danger lurking everywhere. At home in Canada, she's not like this. At home, she even let Gordo have an insect collection in his room. She's changed. There's something going on with her, and I don't know what it is. She makes us brush our teeth with boiled water and won't let us go outside in bare feet. In the evenings we have to wear long sleeves because of the mosquitoes, even though it's still ninety degrees outside. She thinks the soldiers standing at the roadblocks are pointing their guns at us. She's convinced that insects will burrow into our toes and our guts and our bloodstreams, and we'll all get sleeping sickness or malaria or dengue fever, or the soldiers will shoot us.

Any kind of spider would be just another danger to her.

Honestly, I think Mom's in way over her head, and she figures the sooner Dad's done his work helping with the elections, the sooner she'll be able to get us all out of here.

There's no freedom for me and Gordo here at all. At home, we walked to school and biked around the neighborhood with our friends. If it was warm, we went to Dairy Queen. In winter, we hung out in each other's rec rooms and listened to Bee Gees records. On weekends we rode the bus across town to see the latest movies, like *Star Wars*.

I bet when *The Empire Strikes Back* comes out, the whole gang will go.

Here, Mom insists we're picked up and dropped off everywhere we go. Honestly, sometimes I feel like I'm a five-year-old on an endless play date. There's no way I'm giving Mom any more reasons to be paranoid by telling her about the spider.

I glare at Gordo as we settle into the car. "Don't say anything," I mouth. He nods and leans back into the seat.

TWO

I'd be in grade seven at home, but here they call it Form One. Gordo's in Class Five. He thinks it's funny that his class has a higher number than mine. Before we came here, I was worried we'd have to go to a school where everything was in a language we didn't know, but Dad explained that because there are so many languages in Ghana, the schools mostly use English. Lucky for me.

When we get to school, I run to my classroom, slide in beside my friend Thema and sit down. Bassam sits behind me and pulls on my ponytail. I keep forgetting to put my hair in a bun so he can't yank it. I want to turn around and slap him, but I don't dare. Sister Mary gives the scariest evil eye I've ever seen, and I've felt the sting of her anger before. I'm determined not to let it happen again.

Sister Mary hasn't liked me since the first day I came to class and she asked me to show everyone where I come from. She rolled down one of the wall maps until it reached almost to the floor. It was a map of the United States, with a sliver of Canada showing across the top. Sister Mary asked me to put a yellow sticker on my hometown, but the map was blank where Victoria should be, like it didn't exist.

"Place your sticker on Vancouver or Seattle, then," she said.

"I'm not from Vancouver or Seattle," I said.

"How about Toronto?" She pointed to Toronto, half a continent away.

"I'm not from Toronto either."

"At least it's in the same country," she said.

All the other maps were covered in stickers. Most were clustered in Ghana, but there were some in Nigeria and Togo, one in Upper Volta and one in Japan. Everyone else got to put a sticker on their home.

"Maybe we can get a map with Canada on it," I said.

Sister Mary's nostrils flared. "Are you refusing to put your sticker on the map, Astrid?" she asked.

I felt my palms prick. This wasn't fair. In a small voice I said, "Yes, Sister Mary." It was such a little thing, a sticker on a map. But it was my right to claim my home.

Sister Mary snapped the map shut. *Oh, good, Astrid*, I thought. *You've been in school for half a day and already the teacher hates you.* I sat back down and stared at the floor. I tried not to catch Sister Mary's eye for the rest of the day. Or any day since.

Today, I'm determined to stay on Sister Mary's good side, even if it means ignoring Bassam as he pulls my hair, so I lean forward out of his reach and sit still.

"Good morning, Sister Mary," the class chants when she walks into the room.

She smiles and says, "Hello, everyone. I hope you had a good weekend."

"Yes, Sister Mary."

We rise and sing the school song and the Ghanaian national anthem.

We have gym today, so we all go to the bathrooms and change into our shorts and T-shirts and sneakers and head outside to the fields. Our feet scuff the packed red earth up into our eyes as we walk. There's a smell of burning grass in the air. I hate gym, and it's way too hot to feel like doing anything, so Thema and I lag behind until Sister Mary says, "Girls, catch up."

She hands out long loops of elastic to the girls and soccer balls to the boys. The boys run to set up the goalposts, and the girls sort through the elastics. I'd never heard of playing elastics before I came here, but all the girls play it, and since it's pretty much like skipping rope, it didn't take me long to learn the game.

"Sister Mary, may I please watch the soccer? It's too hot to jump elastics," I say.

The girls stare, their eyes moving from me to Sister Mary.

"No, you may not," she says, and I know for sure by the tone of her voice that if I say one more thing about it, I'll find myself cleaning chalkboard dust off the erasers all morning, and I certainly won't be on Sister Mary's good side. I turn away from her and choose an elastic.

Thema and I wrap the elastic around our ankles while Harpreet jumps. She gets as high as our thighs before she trips and it's Thema's turn. Harpreet and I put the elastic back down at our ankles, and Thema jumps in. Thema's the best jumper, and she gets as high as our hips before she trips and it's my turn. I start off okay, but I'm not paying enough attention, so I only get as high as their knees before I miss the pattern and am out.

"What's the matter with you?" Harpreet asks as I trade places with her and she goes again, this time with a longer pattern.

I shrug. "I'm hot."

"Me too," says Thema.

"Let's sit down," says Harpreet. She gathers up the elastic and wraps it around her wrist.

"We're not allowed," says Thema.

"We are if we're faint," says Harpreet, and she puffs up her cheeks so they look bloated and blinks her eyes quickly until they start to water.

"Sister Mary," she calls, "I need to sit down, please."

Sister Mary strides over to take a look. Harpreet blinks her eyes some more and sags a little.

"It's so hot, I feel a bit faint," says Harpreet.

Thema and I both pinch our bottom lips with our teeth to keep from laughing, and the effort makes us both sweat and look terrible.

"You girls should know better than to play elastics in the sun. Why aren't you in the shade? Go and sit under the tree until gym's over," says Sister Mary, and she marches back to the soccer field.

"See? Easy," says Harpreet.

As soon as Sister Mary's far enough away, Thema and I let ourselves laugh. The three of us walk to the tree and sit among its exposed roots. We move slowly in case Sister Mary looks back at us. The tamarind pods rustle above us, and the red dirt swirls in eddies around our feet. The shade is soft on our skin.

There are two soldiers at a roadblock on the other side of the wall. One of them is watching the boys playing, and the other seems to have fallen asleep.

I'm still getting used to seeing soldiers on the streets. Ghana's military runs the country, and they have roadblocks all around. We moved here so Dad can help with the elections that are supposed to give Ghana a proper government. The soldiers don't seem to do much but hang out at these roadblocks. I asked Thomas what the roadblocks are for, and he grimaced and said they were just another part of the corruption that's all around.

Normally, I don't mind the soldiers too much, since I don't have to go near them, but I don't like these ones here at school. Having them on the other side of the school wall every day makes me feel like a prisoner. It's like they're watching us all the time. Mom already does enough of that.

"Heads up," calls Bassam as the soccer ball soars over our heads and hits one of the limbs of the tree. A tamarind pod drops to the ground. The soccer ball bounces off the branch and lands on the road, waking the soldier, who snaps to attention.

Everyone freezes.

The woken soldier kicks the ball into the street, but the other one runs after it and catches it with his foot. He juggles it off his boots. We all crowd along the wall to watch.

"Hey, give us our ball back," says Bassam.

It's like the soldier hasn't heard him. He bounces the ball from foot to foot and up onto his chest and back to his feet. On and on he goes, ignoring the boys.

"He's good," Thema says.

"You ask him for it back. He'll give it to you," Bassam whispers, but Thema doesn't say anything.

"What's going on?" Sister Mary says as she joins us at the wall. She elbows her way through the boys.

"Is that one of our balls?" she asks in a low voice.

We nod. I wait for her to call out to the soldier, who still hasn't taken any notice of us, but instead she says, "Everyone back to the classroom."

"Awww…It's still gym," says Bassam, but Sister Mary cuts him off.

"Come along," she says, and there's a sharpness in her voice that startles me.

"What's that all about?" I whisper to Thema as we walk back to the classroom, but she shrugs her shoulders and says, "I don't know."

"It's weird that Sister Mary is scared of a soldier," I say.

"Yeah," says Thema.

When we get back to the classroom, Bassam's in such a bad mood that he yanks my ponytail so hard it hurts my forehead.

"Ouch," I call out.

He laughs and reaches out to pull it again, but I say, "Get away!" and lean forward so he can't reach.

Sister Mary spins around. "Astrid," she snaps. We're not allowed to speak out of turn in her class. Bassam winks at me. I glare at him, and unfortunately, that's the moment Sister Mary catches my eye.

I sigh, because I know I've done it again.

"Astrid, sit up straight and pay attention," Sister Mary says.

"He started it," I say.

Sister Mary says, "*Whosoever shall smite thee on thy right cheek, turn to him the other also.*"

I don't know what that means, but I know it sounds unfair, and I also know that Bassam started it. It's not my fault Sister Mary is in a bad mood. Bassam chuckles behind me and I want to slap him, I really do, but instead I sit up straight, look forward and try, once again, to stay out of Sister Mary's line of sight for the rest of the day.

THREE

Gordo whines. "Please? Why can't I go with you?"

"Because only your mother and I were invited. I don't think the family across the street has kids. Listen to Astrid. She's in charge while we're gone," says Dad. It's Saturday afternoon, and Dad and Mom are going to the neighbors' house for drinks. Piper has fallen asleep, and Abena, our housekeeper, has agreed to keep her ear open for her while Mom and Dad go out. I don't know why Gordo is whining to go with them, but it's driving me nuts.

"We won't be too long. You know the rules," Dad says. Of course we know the rules. Mom drills them into us every morning.

When Mom and Dad have left, I go upstairs, put my Olivia Newton-John tape on and lie down. It's so refreshing, lying under the air conditioner, and luckily, the power has stayed on for a few days, so the room is cool. I lie there and think about home, about biking to the water park and getting drenched in a shower of cool, clean water. There's nothing like that here, and even if there were, Mom would never let us go. She'd be afraid we'd get cholera from the water.

I wish I knew what was going on with her. Before we got here, Mom said she was planning to buy tribal cloth at the local market and sew me and Piper new dresses. She talked about finding someone to teach her how to cook traditional Ghanaian food. She even said she would take Gordo to a professional soccer game. None of those things have happened. Now she seems scared of everything. That's not the Mom I remember.

I miss the old Mom.

There's a rustle outside the window. I can't make out what it is, so I sit up and peer through the louvers. At first I don't understand what I'm seeing, but then I do. Gordo's climbing out his window and down the pawpaw tree that grows against the wall.

I slam my hands against the window slats. "Gordo," I yell, but either he doesn't hear me because of the air conditioners or he's ignoring me.

I can't believe it. Rule number one is, don't leave the house unless you get permission from Mom or Dad or another adult. Also, there are bars across the windows. How on earth did he squeeze through the louvers and bars?

"Gordo," I call again. He's almost on the ground and he'll be gone in a second, so I spring out of bed and rush down the stairs.

"Gordo's escaping—I'm going after him. I'll be right back," I yell to Abena. There's no answer, so I hurry into the kitchen, but she's not there. The kitchen door slams behind me as I dash out to the laundry area, but she's not there either. I can't see Gordo anymore, so I sprint to the end of the driveway and look down the street. There he is, easy to spot. The only kid with white skin and yellow hair in the middle of a crowd of dark bodies. They leap across a ditch. I know what they're doing: having a contest. Gordo loves contests.

"Gordo, stop," I shout. When he hears me, he and the other kids run down the street away from me.

"Gordo," I call again, but he doesn't stop. He is going to be in trouble if Mom finds out. Big trouble. And since I'm supposed to be in charge, so will I. "Abena," I shout, "I'm going down the street after Gordo." Then I sprint after him.

The boys run to the end of the street and into a field. I almost turn around, but then the boys skip back onto the street on the other side of the field, and I plunge into the tall grasses to catch up with them.

"Gordo!" I scream in my harshest voice.

He doesn't answer or even turn around.

"You are in so much trouble."

He skips across a ditch.

"Dad's going to string you up by the thumbs."

Nothing.

"Gordo, get your butt back here or I'm telling!"

The boys laugh.

Where is Gordo going? And what if there are soldiers on the way? I haven't seen any in our neighborhood, but if anyone knows where to find them, it's Gordo. It would be just like him, always finding something dangerous and heading straight for it.

I push that thought out of my mind.

The boys keep going until the road peters out in scrub, and then they push right into the bushes. I'm scratched and sweaty and muddy, and I don't like the look of the woody, thorny branches, but I've followed the boys this far. I can't turn around now.

I push aside a branch with my arm and step into the scrub. Immediately I'm caught in a vine, and every time I try to pull away it hooks onto another part of me, until finally the sticky green leaves are wrapped around my chest and arms. My breath comes sharply.

I try to pull away again, but more of the vine twists itself around me. "Damn," I say. I'm determined not to panic. It's only a vine. I yank on it again, this time more sharply, and some of the leaves tear off me. I grab handfuls of it and pull.

By the time I'm free, I can't hear Gordo or the other boys anymore, but I can hear a deep rumbling, like thunder. It grows louder by the second, and the air twists around and throws dust into my eyes.

A plane closes in on me.

It seems to take up the whole sky.

I run, but I'm disoriented and don't know where to go, so I run away from the noise. I stumble through the scrub until the plane is so close, it's almost on top of me. With a scream, I throw myself against a small rise in the ground.

The plane passes over me.

Above me, on the top of the rise, Gordo and the other boys stand with their arms akimbo. As the plane flies over their heads, the wind lifts the boys like leaves, and they tumble down the hill toward me, screaming and laughing. Gordo lands next to me.

"Astrid! What are you doing?" he shouts. I open my mouth, but no noise comes out.

"Don't tell," says Gordo. "Please don't tell." The other boys hang back, but Gordo stands in front of me and waits for me to speak.

My heart races, and my whole body shakes. "Are you stupid?" I shout at him. "Do you have any idea how dangerous this is?"

"It's not," he says. "The planes are too high to hit us."

I can't believe what I'm hearing. "You've done this before?"

"Yeah, but it's not dangerous."

"Gordo…" I don't know what to say.

"Don't tell. Please don't tell."

I look at him standing there covered in dry grass and leaves. How could he be such an idiot?

"I won't do it again, I promise." Gordo's good at pleading. He does it a lot.

I rub my hands up and down my legs to stop them from shaking. "Why shouldn't I tell? What else have you been doing?"

"Nothing, I promise. Most of the time, we watch lizards or see who can spit farthest. Nothing dangerous— I promise."

"That's a lot of promising," I say.

"Please," he says.

What good would telling do? I suddenly have this image of Mom locking Gordo and me in a room and refusing to let us out again until we agree to wear space suits to protect us, like the astronauts.

"I won't tell, but only if this is the last time you do it," I say.

"Promise," says Gordo.

"Pinky swear?"

"Pinky swear." We wrap our pinkies together and shake.

"We'd better get home before Mom and Dad do," I say.

Before we leave, I brush off my shorts and peer over the top of the hill. Ahead of me is the airport runway, and at the far end, the plane, with people walking past soldiers and into the airport.

We jog home. Gordo lags behind a few times, but I yank his arm and hurry him up. We're just through the gates when we hear Dad's voice call out, "Joanne, they're here." He stands at the front door, holding Piper tightly, and the look on his face tells us we're in big trouble. Mom runs out of the house. She's crying.

"Where were you? What if something had happened?" she says.

Gordo opens his mouth, but I glare at him and he shuts up.

"We were out walking, Mom. It's so hot in the rooms." I hate lying, but I hope my red face will make Mom think I'm telling the truth about it being too hot. "I need a glass of water to cool down," I say.

"Not so fast, young lady," says Dad. He can tell I'm lying. He always knows. "The air-conditioning's on in your room."

My red face burns even brighter, until it's so hot I think I might faint. Now I really do need to lie down or drink some water.

"You're grounded until further notice. You know how much your mother worries. All you had to do was tell Abena that you were hot and you wanted to go outside," Dad says.

"I did tell her," I say, but even that's not quite true. I shouted at her, but I didn't wait to see if she had heard.

"Think of the position you put Abena in. Your mother was upset with her when we came home and you two were gone."

Gordo hangs his head.

Dad and I stare at each other.

"It's not fair. I was running after Gordo," I say, but Dad's face doesn't change.

Mostly what I want to do right now is turn around and walk right back down the driveway and up the street to the airport and onto a plane out of here. I want to go back home, and I want life to be the way it used to be.

"Grounded," I say in a small voice.

"Until I say otherwise," says Dad.

"What about Gordo?" I ask.

"Gordo too," he says. "But you're the one who was supposed to be in charge. Astrid, you're old enough to understand that things are tense right now. You know the soldiers are on edge, what with the elections coming."

Soldiers, soldiers, soldiers. They're becoming Dad's excuse for everything. He thinks he knows all about them.

"But…" I want to tell him that it's Gordo's fault. I promised Gordo I wouldn't tell about the planes, so I don't, but the unfairness tears at me. As we walk into the house, I try to catch Gordo's eye, but he refuses to look at me.

This is his fault, and he knows it.

FOUR

On Monday, Mom picks us up right after school and drives us home. She doesn't even come a little late like she usually does so that I can hang out with Thema. I slide into the back seat, behind her, where I don't have to look at her face.

"Good afternoon, Astrid," she says, but I scowl and stare out the window for the whole drive home.

As we walk in the door, Mom says, "Anyone for an egg-salad sandwich?" but I storm up the stairs, pulling my uniform off as I go. We have some kind of eggs for lunch every day. Mom says eggs are the only things that are reliably available, but I'm sick of them. I never want to eat another egg-salad sandwich again. Plus the last thing I want is to sit at the table listening to Gordo and Mom chew.

I throw my uniform against the wall and count all the things I hate about being here. Number one is being grounded. That never happened at home, because at home, Mom wasn't watching our every move. We had freedom at home.

Number two is getting blamed for everything. Gordo's the one being stupid. All I'm doing is trying to watch out for him. It's his fault we got grounded.

Three, having to hide things from Mom. I hate doing that, but if she's going to be so paranoid, I'm going to have to.

Four is being stared at every time I leave the house.

Five, soldiers.

Six, when the power goes out—like now—and my room feels like a sauna.

Seven, Sister Mary's evil eye.

Eight, Bassam pulling my hair.

Nine, spiders, snakes and mosquitoes.

Ten, nasty-tasting malaria pills.

Eleven, having to boil water before we drink it.

I keep going until there are thirty-five things on my list. When I finally run out of things I hate about Ghana, I lie down and fall asleep.

Later in the afternoon, I take my book outside and pull a chair under a tree. I'm reading *The Dark is Rising*, one of my favorites—at least it was the first three times

I read it. I've finished up to *The Grey King* in the series, and I can't wait to read *Silver on the Tree*, but we don't have it with us, and it's not like we can walk down to the store and buy a copy. We'll have to wait until Aunt Alice sends it in a care package. If she sends it. That's another thing for my list. Not being able to buy new books.

At least there's shade under the tree, and at least it's away from Mom, but it doesn't take me long to realize I can't read this book for a fourth time, so I put it down on the chair and walk around to the other side of the house to see what Gordo's up to. That's how bored I am.

The boys Gordo was playing with yesterday mill about under the laundry hanging on the line. There are five of them, all about Gordo's age, and they stand around barefoot with snotty noses and play stupid games like who can shoot a rock farthest with his slingshot and who can make the biggest splat on the pavement with his spit. It's gross, and if I had anything else to do, I would do it. Even seeing them makes me all mad again, because it's so unfair that Gordo has kids to boss around and I'm stuck on my own. I know these are just boys who live in huts along the street—they're not real friends from school—but still.

They're competing now to see who can jump farthest off the wall of the laundry area attached to the side of the house. Two of them already stand in place, one slightly farther out than the other, and they watch Gordo as he swings his arms back and forth before he leaps.

"Astrid, watch," he says, and he pumps his arms way back and jumps.

"Aww," he says when he doesn't go as far as either of the other boys, but he stands his ground. I half expect him to try and slide an inch or two past them, but he doesn't. Instead, he says something I don't understand.

"What did you say?" I ask.

"It's Kwame's turn." He points to a boy climbing up onto the wall.

"Were you speaking Twi?" I ask.

"Yes," he says.

I'm amazed. I've learned a few phrases in Twi, but only things like "hello" and "how are you." Nothing like what Gordo said.

Kwame jumps and lands even closer to the house than Gordo. He crosses his arms and pouts. Then the next two boys take their turns. They're about to declare a winner when I say, "Wait—my turn" and clamber up onto the wall.

When I stand up on the wall, the boys stare at me like they've never seen a girl jump off a wall before. One of them is actually gaping at me. Well, they probably never *have* seen a girl jump off a wall before. Certainly not a white girl with a blond ponytail. I pump my arms back and forth, then leap as far as I can.

"Ha," I say when I land a good foot farther than the boys.

"Oh, go away," says Gordo, and he grabs the arm of the boy next to him and tugs. The boy glares at me, and I give him my ice-queen look until Gordo tugs at him again and all six of them run away.

Good riddance. Jumping off walls is kid stuff.

When the boys are gone, there's nothing to do but go back to my book under the tree. Thomas reaches the tree at the same time as I do. He slides down the trunk into a squat, picks up his whittling knife and turns on his shortwave radio. Thomas carves animals out of wood. Whenever he takes a break from gardening, I find him here with a knife in his hand.

"What are you making?" I ask.

He shaves away a tiny piece of wood from his carving, then hands the animal to me. It's a tiny giraffe. Its long neck curves with the bend of the wood, and its legs are as spindly and awkward as a newborn foal's.

"It's beautiful," I say.

"It needs to be polished," he says, taking it back from me. He runs his hand over the wood as if he can smooth its roughness that way.

"No. It's perfect how it is."

He smiles when I say that but keeps rubbing at the wood.

"Will you make one for Piper?" I pick up another piece of wood lying next to the tree. This one is lighter and wider. He hasn't started carving it yet.

"A hippopotamus," he says. "You can't break a hippo."

I laugh. "Perfect," I say. "What do you do with them all?"

"My wife Esi sells them at Makola market."

I almost drop the piece of wood. Thomas has a wife?

"Really?" I ask, then blush. I shouldn't be surprised. Thomas is handsome and nice, and he's pretty old. Twenty-five at least. It makes sense that he's married. It's just that he spends all his time at our house. I've never thought about whether he has a family of his own.

"Really what?" he asks.

"Nothing."

Abena bangs out the kitchen door with two mugs of tea in her hand. She offers one to Thomas. "Are you still grounded?" she asks, even though it's only been two days. Obviously, she doesn't know Mom. Being grounded could last forever.

"Yes," I say.

"I bet your mom won't mind if you go shopping with Abena," Thomas says.

"Where are you going?" I ask Abena.

"I have coupons for soap, so we'll go and get some later today," she says. She takes a sip of her tea, then adds, "You can come if you want."

Even though I want to go and do something, standing in line to buy soap sounds even more boring that staying here, so I say, "No, thank you" as politely as I can.

Abena and Thomas both laugh. Thomas gulps down his tea, hands Abena his mug and stretches. "Back to work," he says, and both of them go off, leaving me sitting under the tree alone.

FIVE

Being grounded is driving us all crazy. Even Mom. I think she thought it would be good to have me and Gordo around all the time, but one night I overhear her and Dad talking and she uses words like *underfoot* and *moping*. What did you expect, Mom? It's been two weeks so far. When will this end?

It's not so bad for Gordo, because he goes outside and plays with his slingshot and watches spiders spin webs, and most days the kids from the street creep up the driveway into the yard without Mom noticing. But my friends live farther away, so I'd have to arrange for them to be driven over, and Mom always says no, not while I'm grounded.

Most of the time I sit outside under the tree and watch the clouds. I'm bored, bored, bored. Sometimes Thomas comes and sits with me when he takes his breaks. Right now he's whittling an elephant. Piper's hippo lies at his side. So far it has a head with a big mouth and tiny ears, and front shoulders and legs. The back hasn't been carved yet.

"I like Piper's hippo best," I say, picking it up. The wood is still rough. "I like how fat it is."

"Me too," says Thomas. He chooses a scrap of sandpaper from a pile and rubs it up and down the tiger's back.

"Who's that for?" I ask.

"An American lady," he says.

"What American lady? How does she know you make animals?"

"Just an American lady. She saw some of my animals at Esi's market stall and ordered this and a kingfisher." He bends closer to his work as he rubs the sandpaper around the eyes until they become smooth and round.

"When will you finish Piper's hippo?" I ask.

"When I have some spare time," he says.

"Can't you do it first? It's almost done."

"I have to do these first," he says.

"Why?"

Thomas lets the tiger fall into his lap. "Because the American lady is going to pay for these animals."

Thomas's voice is gentle, but I blush all the same. I've never thought of paying him for the hippo. I don't know where to look, so I study my hands until Thomas picks up the tiger and sands it again.

"I'll finish the hippo soon, I promise," he says. He lays the tiger down next to the hippo and stands up and stretches. "Do me a favor, Asteroid—take my teacup in to Abena? I need to get back to work," he says.

When I nod he says, "Thanks" and walks away to the other side of the house. The tiger sits on a piece of cloth. Its eyes stare at me, and I stare back at them until I can't stand it anymore. I throw a handful of grass over the tiger's head and leave.

When I come back from taking in Thomas's teacup, Mom's sitting in the chair under the tree with Thomas's animals and tools beside her while Piper wanders around with a stick. Mom smiles as I come out of the house and says, "Astrid, will you keep an eye on Piper for a while, please? I'm going to the market for some fruit." I want to say no, because I'm still so mad at Mom, but Piper grins her big grin and I say yes. It's better than sitting out here alone anyway.

After Mom leaves, Piper pokes her stick at flowers and dirt and little sandy mounds in the yard. After a while, she plops down and uses her hands to poke around instead.

I stare at the clouds and think about what Thomas said. Should I pay him for Piper's hippo? Even though I knew Esi sells Thomas's animals, I never really thought about Thomas making money from his animals. He already has a job gardening at our house. Why would he need to do both? It seems wrong to pay for the hippo. What if he's insulted if I offer to pay him? I'd have to ask Mom for some money. Maybe Thomas wouldn't like that.

Gordo limps around the house and plunks himself next to me under the tree.

"What happened to you?" I ask.

He stretches out his leg and shows me a scrape along his knee. "I fell," he says. His fingers pick at the blood dried along the edges of the cut.

"Gordo!" I yank his fingers away. "You need to put some Mercurochrome on that."

Piper shrieks. I leap to my feet, knocking over my chair. Piper is sitting in the grass, ants crawling all over her legs. Her mouth is open, but no noise comes out. Then she takes a breath and screams again.

I grab Piper and slap at the ants, brushing them off her legs.

"Put her in water," calls Gordo. He's right. Water will wash the ants away. We run into the kitchen and plop Piper into the sink, then splash water over her legs. Piper reaches out to me, still screaming, and I wrap my arms around her. She digs her fingers into my hair. Tiny black dots float around the water.

I swallow hard and try to stay calm.

"Shhh," I say to Piper through my tight throat. I stroke her arms and shoulders until her screaming slows to sobs, then wipe her hair out of her eyes. "It's okay, sweetie. The ants are gone."

Piper gulps and snivels while Gordo and I wash her legs again, and then I pull her out of the sink. Her legs are covered in swollen red spots, each one an ant bite.

"I'm sorry, honey. I'm sorry." I cuddle her, and we rock back and forth until we both calm down. Gordo strokes Piper's hair and sings a little song to her.

When Mom comes home, I'm reading to Piper in her room. Mom's hair is loose and her face is all blotchy red. I figure Gordo's already told her what happened. Then I remember that I never made sure Gordo got the Mercurochrome.

"It happened so quickly. I didn't know," I stammer.

Mom's eyebrows crease together and she says, "What happened?" And it turns out she *didn't* already know.

I tell her, and she listens with this funny scrunched look on her face, then sighs and sinks onto the bed.

"Come here, sweetie," she says to Piper. She holds out her arms to let Piper crawl into them, and the two of them lean back against the wall. She strokes Piper's head, but her eyes have a faraway look in them, like she's thinking about home. I lean in to rest against her arm too, but she says, "Astrid, is this what's going to happen when I leave Piper with you?"

Her words make my breath catch in my throat, and I feel like I'm going to faint.

"I didn't mean for it to happen. I was trying to help Gordo," I say in a tiny voice.

Mom doesn't say anything.

"Mom, that's so unfair."

Mom sighs and says, "I'm sorry, Astrid. I shouldn't blame you." Her voice sounds strained, like it's hard to get the words out of her throat, so when she stretches out her arm, I lean in to her.

Resting with her isn't comforting today.

SIX

On Monday at school, before Sister Mary comes in, Thema and Harpreet show me Harpreet's new camera. It's a Polaroid, and they've brought along pictures they took yesterday when I was at home, grounded. There's one of the two of them in Harpreet's bedroom, and one of Harpreet's dog.

"I wish I'd been there," I say.

"Your mom's so mean, keeping you grounded," says Harpreet.

"Yeah," I say.

Sister Mary comes into the room, so Harpreet hides the camera in her desk, but not before she whispers, "Break."

After we've risen to sing the school song and the national anthem, Sister Mary says, "Today we're going to talk about the elections."

Bassam's hand shoots up.

"Yes, Bassam?" Sister Mary says.

"Why are we going to talk about the elections when we can't vote?"

It's a good question, but Sister Mary turns her evil eye on Bassam and says, "It's an historic moment, Bassam, and it will bring us back to being the Black Star of Africa." She swivels around and picks up a piece of chalk, then writes the words *Black Star* on the board.

Bassam puts his hand up again.

"Yes, Bassam."

Thema and I smirk at each other. Sister Mary sounds like she'd rather not hear from Bassam again.

"My dad says the system we have now works fine."

Sister Mary's mouth turns down, and she looks a little startled.

"Does he?" she says. She turns back to the board. She underlines the words *Black Star,* then says, "Hmph." Kids giggle. We're not used to seeing Sister Mary at a loss for words.

Bassam continues. "He says Ghanaians need the military or money's going to get into the wrong hands."

Thema turns around in her chair and stares at Bassam. Her mouth hangs open like she's about to say something, but then she turns to me and raises her eyebrows. It's hard not to laugh.

Sister Mary calls us back to attention and goes on with her lesson, which is all about democracy and how it makes life better for people. I've heard it all before from Dad, but I still find Bassam's snickering annoying. He sort of gurgles every time Sister Mary talks about how the current system keeps people poor. Once, he whispers, "People get what they deserve." I'm about to put my hand up and tell on him when the bell rings and it's time for break.

Thema, Harpreet and I run to the tamarind tree. Harpreet laughs so hard, she snorts.

"Thema, you should have seen the look on your face when Bassam talked back to Sister Mary." Harpreet imitates Thema by raising her eyebrows and dropping her jaw. She looks dumbfounded.

Thema says, "His dad owns eleven cars."

"Really?" I knew his family was rich, but eleven cars! "What do they do with them?"

Thema shrugs. "Who knows?"

Harpreet pulls the camera out of her pocket and says, "Let's take pictures of him. Maybe we can catch him when he's not looking." Thema and I nod, and we head for the field where the boys play soccer.

"Maybe we'll catch him picking his nose," says Harpreet, and Thema and I laugh.

When we get there, Bassam's showing off with the soccer ball. He bounces it on his feet, up to his chest and back to his feet again. He moves closer and closer to the wall with each bounce, until finally he bounces the ball right over the wall and into the group of soldiers at the roadblock. It's like he does it on purpose. Thema and I stop, and so do all the other boys, but Harpreet runs to the wall and snaps a picture as one of the soldiers waves his arms at us, shouting something in Ga or Twi.

"Harpreet!" I yell. I can't believe she's just done that. I bite the corner of my lip and stand back from the wall, next to Thema. She fumbles for my hand and holds it tight.

Bassam laughs. "It was an accident—honest," he says, still laughing at what he's done.

The soldier walks right to the wall and points at Bassam, then shouts something again.

Bassam backs away, not laughing anymore.

"What did he say?" I ask Thema, but before she can answer, the headmistress storms past us, rushes up to the wall and speaks to the soldier. I can't understand what she's saying, but I can tell from the tone of her voice that she's trying to calm him. The soldier says something back and points at Bassam and then at Harpreet. Thema and I both move closer to Harpreet as the headmistress glances at her, frowning. She turns back to the soldier and says something else. The soldier nods at her and walks away. The headmistress spins around, grabs Bassam by his collar and marches him toward the school building. As she passes Harpreet, she says, "You're next."

Harpreet curtseys. "Yes, ma'am," she says. She holds the photo and the camera behind her back and puts a smile on her face.

No one says anything as the headmistress and Bassam disappear into the office.

As soon as the headmistress closes the door, Harpreet laughs and waves the Polaroid picture in the air. "Look at this," she calls. "That soldier looks retarded, the way his face is all crooked." She speaks loudly, like she's daring the rest of us to look at the photo with her. The boys mill around, scuffing their feet. Thema twists her hair in her fingers and stands closer to me than ever. I glance over the wall to see if the soldier has heard.

"Shut up, Harpreet," one of the boys says, but she laughs at him.

"Are you scared?"

Before he can answer, we hear Sister Mary's voice. "What have you got there, Harpreet?" She's come up behind us, and no one noticed her arrive.

"It's nothing," says Harpreet. She's put the camera and the photo behind her back again. She tries to shove the photo into my hand, but I keep my fist tight.

Sister Mary holds out her hand and says, "I believe it is something. Let me see."

"It's really nothing," says Harpreet.

Thema and I both hold our breath as Harpreet and Sister Mary stare at each other. Then Thema says,

"We were trying out Harpreet's new Polaroid camera, Sister Mary."

"Thank you, Thema," says Sister Mary. She holds her hand out again, and Harpreet brings her arm around and gives the picture to Sister Mary, who takes a deep breath.

"What on earth were you thinking, girls? You need to be very careful flashing that camera around. Don't make the soldiers more nervous than they already are with the elections this close." Her voice isn't angry. Worse, it's scared.

"We're sorry, Sister Mary. We got carried away," says Harpreet. "We didn't mean anything by it."

Sister Mary stares at the picture until I think it's going to melt in her hand. Finally, she holds out her hand for Harpreet's camera.

"You can have this back at the end of the day," she says, "but I don't want to see you girls near this wall again." She starts to turn away, then stops and says, "Go back to the tree and stay there until break is over. Harpreet, you're in for detention. Understood?"

Harpreet sticks her tongue out as Sister Mary walks back to the school. "She's so mean. I can't believe she took my camera away. She's such a cow, an elephant. Sister Mary Elephant." Harpreet flips her long hair over her shoulder and saunters over to the tamarind tree. Thema and I follow her more slowly.

Heat pricks at my fingers and up my arms as I remember the look on the soldier's face when he leaned over the wall and pointed at Bassam.

SEVEN

I'm tired out when I get home from school in the afternoon, but when Mom says, "What's up, honey?" I find I can't tell her what happened with the soldiers. I used to tell her everything, but I don't know how she'd react now. No, I do know how she'd react, and that's what stops me from telling her. I wish she was like she used to be—relaxed and fun.

I play with my food until I notice her staring at me, then eat a big mouthful of egg salad and try to smile.

"You look like you need cheering up, Astrid," she says, and I look up. She's going to say I'm not grounded anymore! But then she says, "Let's go to the market. I haven't been for ages."

I look back down and fidget with my food.

"Oh, it'll be fun," says Mom. Her voice is bright. She reaches across the table and lifts my chin.

"We both need a little cheering up, eh?" she says.

I swallow my food. Mom seems happy today. It's been awhile.

"We'll give Piper a treat. It's been boring for her these days at home with me," Mom says.

"I'm still grounded," I say.

"We won't tell Dad." She gets up and pulls Piper out of her chair, and the two of them dance around the room. Piper laughs and reaches out to me, so I get up and join them.

We take Thomas with us, since Mom is scared to drive in the maze of downtown streets. "We'll be about half an hour," says Mom to Thomas when we get to the market and she's gathering her bags.

Thomas waves goodbye and pulls out a newspaper. He looks so relaxed leaning against the car, I wish I could stay there with him instead of jostling my way through the stalls.

As always, the noise of people bargaining and the smells of fresh spices and rotting fish hit us first. It's dark in the aisles between stalls, but not cool, and the spicy-fishy air makes it hard to breathe. To me the market is like a beehive—so full of motion.

"If we get separated, come back to the car," says Mom.

"I know, Mom." That's what she always says. It's one of the rules. I hike Piper up higher on my hip and trail behind Mom.

Piper's interested in everything and squirms from side to side trying to see. We weave through the stalls, and Mom spends the whole time complaining about how there's so little for sale even though this is a country of farmers. My face burns with embarrassment. Why did she come here if she's going to be like that?

"Mom, a lot of these people can understand English, you know," I say.

She shakes her head and keeps talking to herself.

I hold Piper tight to keep her from jumping down and darting away. There are so many people here, it would be easy to lose her.

A boy comes by with a softly-softly in his arms. We've seen him here before. The softly-softly is so cute, like a cross between a monkey and a sloth, with huge eyes so that it can see at night. Dad says it's a kind of potto, which is like a lemur, and Gordo keeps begging for one. Thomas warned us that they can be vicious, so of course Mom always says no.

I ignore the boy, but he speaks to Piper.

"Baby, you want to pet the softly-softly? So cute, like you." He draws close, and Piper puts out her hand to pet the little animal.

"Don't touch, Piper," I say, but the boy comes closer. He pats the softly-softly on the head and it closes its eyes and licks its lips with its tiny tongue. Piper reaches out again, and I twist away so she can't reach. "It might bite your finger," I say.

"It won't bite—it's almost asleep," says the boy. He holds the animal up so Piper can reach it more easily.

"We don't want it," I say, but he ignores me and holds the softly-softly so that it's almost in Piper's arms.

"Go away," I say. With a scowl at me and a wink at Piper, he finally walks away. Piper whimpers as the softly-softly disappears.

"Mom, I'm taking Piper to get a cold drink," I say.

"Give me a minute," Mom says.

"Please, Mom?"

"Wait." She pays for a handful of tomatoes and puts them in one of her bags.

"We'll be fine, Mom," I say.

"Thank you," she says to the woman, and then she turns to me and says, "Let's go."

Before we can buy a soda, we have to go back to the car to get empty soda bottles to exchange for the full soda bottles at the stall. At first this seemed like a crazy system, but now we're used to it.

People call out to us as they always do when I'm with Piper. I try to ignore them, but they reach out to touch her, and she smiles and giggles at them, which makes them crowd even closer. It's hot as an oven in here, there's no fresh air, and there are people everywhere.

My breath is ragged, and my face feels flushed.

There's something going on at the end of the path we usually take, and there are so many people, we can't get through. Mom leads us down a new path, but there are too many people there too, and in a flash she's gone. I grip Piper tightly, and she cries in my ear. She's so sweaty she's about to slip from my arms, and I'm having a hard time catching my breath. It's all I can do to hold on to her.

It's going to take forever to get to the car!

But then Thomas's voice says, "Astrid, over here," and we follow his voice through the crowd to a stall.

A woman sits next to him on a crate. The cloth of her dress is traditional, but the style is modern, and she has her hair done in a cornrow pattern I've never seen before. She fiddles with the dial on a ghetto blaster. When she hears Blondie, she turns up the volume.

"*One way or another*," she sings along with Blondie. Thomas grins and reaches out to take Piper from me. I sag in relief.

"Astrid, this is my wife, Esi," he says.

I use my T-shirt to wipe the sweat out of my eyes. Esi waves at me and keeps singing. I smile back.

"Where's your mom?" asks Thomas.

"We lost her. She'll go to the car. We should go too. That's where we said we'd meet," I say.

Thomas sits Piper on his stool and says, "You stay here and have a drink. I'll go get your mom."

Esi dances over to me. I join her, moving my feet in the space between the crate and the wall. "*I'm gonna getcha getcha getcha getcha one way or another,*" we shout into the crowded air. My breathlessness is gone now. Piper claps and we dance and sing until the song's over.

"Phew, I'm thirsty," I say. I'm sweating all over, and my shirt sticks to my back.

"I have some drinks back here," says Esi, reaching under a crate at the back of the stall.

"Great," I say, but then I remember. Mom will have a fit if we drink something that doesn't come in a sealed bottle. It's the only way to be safe, she always says. But I don't want to be rude. It's generous of Esi to offer me a drink—it's not like she can turn on a tap and have drinking water come out.

I'm still thinking about how to say no when she stands up and hands me a Coke. "There's a bottle opener here somewhere," she says. The Coke's warm, and its strong taste burns my mouth, but it feels good anyway. I give a sip to Piper, but she scrunches up her nose and coughs. Esi pats her on her back and says, "Water would be better, but we'll get a coconut for you, baby." I should have known Esi wouldn't offer us unboiled water. Thomas has probably told her what Mom's like.

I relax and look around. The stall is filled with wooden animals.

"These are Thomas's?" I ask.

"Aren't they beautiful?" says Esi.

"This is where you sell them?"

Esi nods. "When we've sold enough, we'll use the money to get a house. That's our plan."

I can picture it. A little house with Esi singing inside and Thomas gardening outside.

The stall shelves are full. There's a family of elephants—two big ones and five little ones, each holding onto the tail of the one in front of it. There are two giraffes, their necks entwined, and a growling hyena. There are birds too—something with long legs, and several egrets. Crocodiles open their mouths wide, and antelope bend to drink. Each animal is set in a scene, next to a pond made of blue cloth or under a tree made of a branch or soaring through the air on coat hangers. It's like being in a tiny natural history museum.

"This is beautiful," I say.

"Thomas lives for his animals," says Esi.

Thomas arrives then and says, "Your mom's not happy with you. We'd better get back to the car."

My good mood evaporates, and I want to scream. Mom doesn't trust me at all anymore. Not even to find my way through the market to the car.

I stand abruptly. "Bye, Esi, it was nice to meet you," I say as we leave.

"You too, Astrid," she says.

Thomas kisses Esi, and she takes a long time letting go of his hand, as if she doesn't want him to leave, but he pulls away and says to me, "Let's go before your mom gets more worried." He throws Piper up onto his shoulders so she's riding high and leads the way back toward the car. I trail behind a bit so that I can stop being upset before I see Mom.

"Oh, thank goodness," Mom says when we reach the car. Her voice is breathless, and she drops the two bags she's holding and grabs Piper from Thomas. Oranges and tomatoes roll on the dusty ground.

"I lost you," she says.

"We were fine. I could have found my way," I say.

She hugs Piper, who squirms in the heat of her arms. Thomas picks up Mom's bags, and together we put the oranges and tomatoes back into the bags.

When I stand up, Mom's crying and kissing Piper like she's a long-lost baby she hasn't seen in months. Piper looks as if she's about to scream, so I say, "Mom, it's okay. We were with Thomas."

She doesn't seem to hear me, and she clutches Piper closer to her chest.

"Mom." I reach over and grab her arm so she has to pay attention. "Let's get into the car. It's too hot."

Thomas has already opened the doors, and Mom lets me lead her to the front seat. As soon as she sits down, I take Piper from her and the two of us crawl into the back seat. Thomas noses the car away from the parking lot and turns on the air-conditioning. The cool air washes over us like relief, but there's a knot inside my stomach that doesn't go away, especially when Mom leans her head against the back of her seat and covers her face with her hands.

EIGHT

On the weekend, Dad finally gives in about us being grounded, and we all go to the beach with Thema's family. Thank goodness. Three weeks of being grounded was way too long. In the morning, Dad runs around the house organizing us. He pops his head into my room and says, "Hat, flip-flops, cover-up, bathing suit."

"Yeah, Dad, I know."

He grins and backs out of the room, and I hear him give the same list to Gordo next door. I pull on my bathing suit and then a T-shirt and shorts over top.

Mom wafts into the room wearing a flowery thing that covers her from neck to toe. When I laugh, she twirls. "Fabulous, eh?" She looks happy, so I say, "Yep. Fabulous."

The drive to the beach is long and dusty, and there are lots of roadblocks where we have to hand over a bribe of a few cedis before we can drive through, so by the time we get there, we all want to run into the waves. When I see the curve of the beach in front of us, I pull off my T-shirt and shorts so I can run out as soon as Dad parks the car.

Mom passes back a bottle of sunscreen. "Goop up," she says.

Gordo and I roll our eyes. Most people use baby oil, so they can get a tan, but we have to cover up with sunscreen so we don't.

"Do I have to?" says Gordo.

"Yes," says Mom without even turning around.

"How come?" Gordo asks.

"Because I said so."

"That's not a good reason."

Gordo and Mom can go on like this for ages, and it drives me crazy. Doesn't Gordo know he'll never win?

"Put it on," I say. I grab the bottle from him and pour some into my hand. I rub it over my body and face and hand the bottle back to Gordo. "It doesn't hurt, you know."

Gordo snatches the bottle from me and pours some into his hand, then rubs it furiously onto his face and arms. When he's done, he slouches in his seat. *So what?* I think. *Let him sulk if he wants to.*

Dad pulls the car onto the sand and parks next to Mr. Ampofo's car. Thema and her brother, Ebo, run to our car.

"Race you to the water," says Thema as Gordo and I climb out, and the four of us run toward the waves.

"Wait," shouts Mom, and she runs after us, waving hats in the air. No one on the whole beach is wearing a hat, but Mom insists we put them on. Gordo and I take ours, then wait until Mom's back is turned before we toss them onto the sand.

Gordo and Ebo play a game where one of them squats in the water and the other climbs onto the squatter's knees. When the squatter stands, the other person flies up and lands in the water. I try it with Gordo, then with Thema, but it works better if the squatter's taller than you, so Thema asks Ebo to give her a ride. He bends down and holds out his hand so she can climb onto his knees. When he stands, she flies way up into the air and lands with a splash next to me.

"Try it with him," Thema splutters when she comes to the surface. I blush at the thought and turn away, but Ebo calls out, "Come on, Astrid," so I swim underwater for a second, then head over to where he's standing.

"Are you ready?" he says. He holds out his hand. I put my hand in his and step onto his bent legs. He grins at me and squats down. His hand grips mine, and then he pushes me upward as he stands, and I hang in the air for a second before splashing deep into the water below.

I splutter and snort and cough as my head surfaces.

"Are you okay?" he asks.

I nod but keep hacking.

"Next time, cover your nose," he says. He pats me on the back as I cough some more.

I nod again, but there isn't going to be a next time. I wade to the shallows and sit on the sand.

Thema comes over and sits down next to me. "Are you okay?" she asks.

I nod.

"Let's get the air mattresses," she says.

"Good idea."

The two of us inflate the mattresses, wade out knee deep, then hop on and float in the gentle waves. Neither of us says anything. It's relaxing, lying here. Our hands trail in the water, and our mattresses rock softly. My mind wanders, and I think about my friends back home and how they're probably sitting in someone's rec room right now, watching TV or listening to records. Or maybe they're all biking around the neighborhood. Usually when I think about them I get sad, but not today. Today the only thing I want to do is lie here and float with Thema.

Thema starts to sing, and I flip over to watch her. She has the most beautiful voice. Mom says she sounds like an African angel. Dad says she could give the opera singer Jessye Norman a run for her money. Thema always talks about going to London when she's older to study voice. She could do it too—she's that good. Her voice is big, even here on the water, and it makes me laugh to watch her face as it fills with the sound she's making. We both giggle as she fills up her chest and finishes the song.

"Sing something from Donna Summer," I say.

She starts a song I haven't heard before. "What is that?" I ask.

"'Hot Stuff.' It just came out. Auntie sent it from London. You have to come over to listen. You have to." She sings the first line again, and I can't help but sit up so I can dance. Thema sits too, and then we both stand and dance around on the wobbly air mattresses.

"Astrid!" Mom's voice carries loudly across the water. I turn and wave at her, but she calls again. "Astrid!" There's something in her voice, even across the water, that makes me sit.

"What's the matter?" Thema says to me.

"I don't know." Mom is waving frantically, so I flop down on the mattress and paddle for shore with Thema right beside me. When the water is knee deep, we both hop off and wade in.

"Come in, please, Astrid. You know you're not supposed to stand on the air mattresses," says Mom. She puts her hand out to take the mattress from me.

"Mom! We were hardly far out at all," I say.

"That's not the point."

"We were only at chest level. If I fell off, I could stand up in the water easily."

"Arguing with me isn't helping, Astrid."

"It's okay, Astrid, we can sit here," says Thema, and the two of us sit down on our mattresses in the shallow water.

Mom stands over us for a minute, then says, "Astrid, the air mattress, please."

"Mom! We're in, like, two inches of water."

She reaches over to take it from me, but I'm a bit too far away, and she stumbles.

"Astrid, you give me that thing right now."

"Why?" I ask. She's being stupid. I *was* going to give it back to her, but now I'm not.

"Astrid, one more word from you and you'll sit in the car for the rest of the day," says Mom. Her face is red, and her voice sounds choked.

"Astrid, it's okay. Give her the mattress. I'll put mine away too," says Thema, but I stare at Mom and pull the mattress farther away. My face burns now, though I'm still in the water. Why is Mom acting like this? She never used to treat me this way. She used to be fun, but now all she ever does is tell me I can't do things. She's done that so many times over the past few weeks.

I'm tired of it.

Thema pulls my mattress out from beneath me and hands it to Mom. "It's not worth it," she whispers. Mom takes the mattress and walks away, and Thema and I go sit back on the sand.

"Your mom seems tired," says Thema.

Thema's so understanding. She always has something nice to say about people. I would have said Mom was crazy or, if I was being more serious, disturbed.

But tired is maybe all that's wrong with Mom. Maybe she's tired out. That doesn't make sense, though, because at home she didn't have Abena to help her and she wasn't exhausted there.

"I'm not sure what's wrong with her," I say.

"She seems…" Thema's voice trails away, and then she says, "Stricter than usual."

"Yeah."

"Ebo brought some boogie boards," says Gordo, running up. "I'm going to try it."

"Yeah, right," I say.

"I am." He stands up and jumps into a surfing pose. It's funny yet not, because I know one hundred percent for certain that Mom will never let him do it. Never.

"You won't be allowed," I say.

Gordo pouts and slams the water with his palm. He falls to the ground and looks like he's about to explode.

Before he can, Thema says, "I know. Let's go buy sun-spots in the village."

Gordo and I both jump up. "Great idea. I'll get some money," I say. Sun-spots are really just frozen orange juice, but they taste so good as they melt in your mouth. Gordo smiles again, and I'm happy not to have to listen to him throw a temper tantrum.

I walk up the beach to where Dad is sitting with Piper under a coconut tree next to the cars. "Dad, can I have some cedis to buy sun-spots?"

Piper claps, and Dad says, "If you take Piper along."

"Sure," I say.

Dad pulls out his wallet and hands me a clump of cedis. I hoist Piper onto my hip.

"You'd better take your hats in case Mom sees you walking down the beach," Dad says. I'm about to protest, but he says, "It's just a hat, Astrid. Please," and the tiredness in his voice makes me agree.

Gordo and Piper and I all shove our hats onto our heads, and I pull a T-shirt over Piper to cover her shoulders. We join Thema and Ebo, and the five of us walk down the beach. We stay low, where the sand is cool and hard. I let Piper down and she holds my hand on one side and Thema's on the other, and we swing her along as we go.

We don't have to go as far as the village because we are greeted by a woman carrying a tray of sun-spots in ice on her head. We all buy one, and I get another for Dad.

"Do you think Mom will want one?" I ask Gordo. He shrugs, so I buy her one too.

I pull away the paper wrapping and hand Piper hers. Within seconds, she's covered in sticky orange juice, but she slurps loudly and grins at us.

"We'd better get back before they melt," says Ebo. He's also bought extras for his parents.

"Race. Last one's a dirty rotten egg," yells Gordo as he sprints across the sand. Ebo and Thema follow, and I swing Piper onto my back and run after them. I'm the slowest, of course. As we get close, Mom runs up to us. When she sees Piper, her hand flies to her mouth and her eyes widen in shock.

"What on earth have you done?" she asks. She yanks Piper out of my arms and uses her towel to scrub at Piper's mouth.

"We bought sun-spots. I have ones for you and Dad," I say.

"How could you, Astrid? Those sun-spots, who knows where they're made? Or how?"

I stare at her.

"What were you thinking, giving one to Piper?" She wrestles the rest of the sun-spot out of Piper's fist.

Piper wails.

"Mom?" I glance at Piper. Tears are pouring down her face. "Piper's had them before. You know she has," I say.

Gordo stares at Mom and then shouts, "You're crazy!"

"Don't be so dramatic, Gordo," says Mom.

Gordo flings himself to the ground and flails his arms and legs. He's ready to have that temper tantrum now. Ebo steps back so he doesn't get kicked.

"It's true though," I say.

Mom's lips tighten and I know I'm on dangerous ground, but I'm tired of Mom always saying no when everyone else says yes. Maybe there's something wrong with her, but why does she have to take it out on us?

"It's not my fault that you're irresponsible, Astrid," she says.

The unfairness of her words slaps me so hard my eyes sting, and I gasp. "Irresponsible?"

"Letting Gordo out of the house when we were away is one example. Letting Piper get bitten by ants is another. Buying sun-spots made out of God knows what kind of water…"

I'm breathless, and I can only stare at her.

If Gordo was gearing up for a tantrum before, he goes still as a rock now. He opens his mouth, but no voice comes out.

Ebo says, "My mom has always let us have them, ever since we were little."

"Well, that's your family," says Mom. Her mouth is a fine, thin line.

"Come on, Thema, we'll let Astrid and Gordo talk with their mom," says Ebo.

He and Thema walk down toward the water where their parents are swimming. Thema turns back to look at me, but I look away, because I know what the expression on her face will be, and I don't want to see it.

NINE

It takes Mom a couple of days to get back to normal, but by Tuesday she seems more or less okay. Not her old self, but not completely crazy either. She whistles as she rounds us all up, tells us the rules and hustles us into the car to go to school. I don't say anything about the weekend—I sure don't want to risk being grounded again—and I hope Mom was only temporarily stressed.

School is its normal boring self. Sister Mary drones on about Ghanaian geography, and Bassam tries to pull my hair. The only thing that's a bit exciting is when Bassam tries to talk to the soldiers over the wall, and Sister Mary grabs him by the collar and pulls him away. I don't think Sister Mary knows I'm sitting under the tree and can hear them, because she says, "Honestly, Bassam, if you were anyone else's son you'd be expelled for saying something like that. Now stop goading the soldiers and keep your opinions to yourself."

Bassam hangs his head and says, "Yes, Sister Mary," but after she leaves, he laughs and calls to the boys, "Did you see that?" Something about the tone of his voice makes me shiver.

It's a relief when school is over for the day and we can go home.

Mom's still cheery when she picks us up, and she chats on the way home about some new plant she and Thomas are trying out in the garden. We eat scrambled eggs for lunch, and afterward, Mom puts Piper down for her nap.

I go outside to read under the tree for a bit while the household is quiet. It's a little cooler today, and there are clouds in the sky. It might even rain. Thomas comes by, holding something behind his back, and when he reaches me, he says, "Guess which hand."

"Right," I say.

He holds out his right hand. It's wrapped around a bundle, which he places in my lap.

"What is it?"

"Open it and see." He leans against the tree.

The bundle is a piece of cloth draped around something hard. I feel it, then say, "Oh, it's Piper's hippo!"

Thomas grins. "Do you think she'll like it?"

I pull the cloth off and run my hand over the smooth surface of the carving. The hippo is smaller than I expected, all round ears and snout and bum. It has stubby legs and pin-prick eyes. It seems to be smiling. "It's beautiful," I say.

"I made it small for Piper to hold," says Thomas. He takes it from me and cradles it in his hand. "See?"

"She'll love it," I say.

"You can give it to her when she wakes up," he says.

"You should give it to her."

"No, Asteroid, you should." He hands me back the hippo and wraps my hand around it.

I don't know what to say. Should I offer to pay him? Should I ask him him to give it to Piper so she knows he made it? Before I can answer my questions, Thomas says, "It's a new model for me. I think people will like this one."

It makes me feel better to know he will be able to sell other hippos.

I run my thumb across the smooth wood one more time, then say, "Thank you, Thomas. It's really special. She'll love it."

Dad comes home a few minutes later with Mr. Ampofo, Thema's dad. Their faces are serious when they walk through the door, and Dad says, "Astrid, where's your mother?"

before he even says hello. I point to the living room, and the two of them march in. I follow, but Dad says, "We need to speak to your mother privately," and he closes the door.

I'm caught between being angry and being curious, so I stand next to the door and put my ear to it in case I can hear something, but I can't.

"Damn," I whisper, and after I try one more time, I go upstairs to change out of my uniform. When I come back down the stairs, Dad and Mr. Ampofo and Mom are standing in the doorway. They haven't seen me, so I stop and listen to what they're saying.

"It will be fine, Joanne. Come tonight and we'll talk more," says Mr. Ampofo. He smiles at Mom, but she says, "I'm not sure we should be out on the roads. Richard, what do you think?"

"It will be fine, Joanne," Dad says.

"But the kids. I don't want the kids going anywhere they don't have to. I want to know where they are at all times," Mom says.

"Joanne, I think you're overreacting. The man's in jail. It's over," says Dad.

Mom laughs a not-amused laugh and says, "Still."

Her face is pale, and with shock I realize that she's really scared.

Dad must see it too, because he says, "Fine. We'll go tonight, and then for a day or two we'll keep the kids at home except for when they're at school. But really, it's over and it's all fine."

Thema's dad leaves then, and Mom and Dad stand together at the doorway. I make a lot of noise coming down the rest of the stairs so they'll think I just got there.

"How come Thema's dad was here? What's going on?" I ask.

Dad glances at Mom, then says, "Nothing to worry about. A soldier tried to take over the government, but he failed and it's over. We're going to Thema's for dinner, so bring your bathing suit."

"Oh," I say. Suddenly I have so many questions. "How does a soldier take over a government? What does that mean? What does it mean that he failed? Is the government still the same government? Why did he do that? Aren't there about to be elections?"

Dad holds his hand up to stop my words. "Astrid, I really don't have the answers to all those questions. Now, I'm thirsty and your mother needs to lie down. We'll talk later. Go and tell Gordo we're going to the Ampofos' for dinner." He takes Mom's arm. Her face is set in a mask of fear.

"Dad," I say, but he mouths the words "Not now" and nods meaningfully at Mom. I back away. I've never seen a look like that on Mom's face, and it makes something deep in my stomach fall, as if the ground I thought I was standing on suddenly isn't there anymore.

"Dad?" But he's not listening to me. He leads Mom down the hallway, and she holds on to him like she needs his support to stay on her feet. I reach my hand out to the wall and lean into its solidity.

Evening takes a long time to come. I try to talk to Dad again, but he locks himself in the study and doesn't answer when I knock. I try to phone Thema, but there's no dial tone. So I head outside to look for Thomas, but Abena tells me he went home early today. The only thing I can do is sit under the tree and bite my fingernails while I wait.

When Mom and Dad and Gordo come out of the house to go to Thema's, I search Mom's face, but she smiles at me and hands me Piper before she climbs into the car.

"How are you feeling, Mom?" I ask.

"Fine, sweetie. How are you?" she says. I glance over the top of the car at Dad. He shakes his head at me, so I climb into the back seat next to Gordo.

At Thema's, about a dozen parents are pacing, while a whole lot of kids race from house to house. Thema lives in a gated compound, so there are always lots of people around, but not like this. If it weren't for the looks on the adults' faces, this would be a party. Mom makes a beeline for Thema's mom, who hugs her and says, "Are you holding up okay?"

Mom nods and seems about to reply, but then she glances around and notices me and says, "Astrid, go and find Thema."

"Fine. Don't tell me, then," I mutter, but not loudly enough for them to hear.

Thema's in her bedroom changing when I find her.

"Bring your bathing suit?" she asks.

I lift my shirt to show my bathing suit underneath. It's an old one-piece covered in Canadian flags. I wish I had a pretty bikini like Thema's orange-and-pink one, but Mom doesn't believe in bikinis, so red-and-white maple leaves it is. I'm sweating like mad with the suit on under my clothes. When Thema's ready, we run from her room and jump into the pool. Ebo's already there, playing water polo with some other boys.

"Heads up," he calls just before a polo ball smacks into the side of my head.

I wail as tears come to my eyes.

"Are you okay?" Thema and Ebo crowd around me. Ebo takes my arm and leads me to the side of the pool. Even with my head throbbing, I can feel every inch of his hand on my arm.

"You better get out for a minute," he says.

"I'm okay," I say, but I let Thema guide me to the shallow end, and we sit together on the steps until the throbbing subsides. Gordo and a bunch of younger kids cannon-ball into the pool. It's not meant for this many people, and there's hardly room to move. Every second or so, someone jostles me.

"How come there are so many people here?" I ask Thema.

"Dad called a meeting and told everyone from work to come tonight," she says.

"Because of the man who tried to take over the government?" I ask.

"He said *there are things to discuss.*" Thema's an amazing mimic, and she even looks like her dad as she tucks in her chin and wags her head like he does. I laugh. I'm glad we're here. Thema and Ebo seem relaxed, and being with them makes me feel better too.

Gordo cannonballs right into an older boy, and a splashing fight breaks out. Chlorine stings my eyes as the spray hits me in the face.

"Let's go to your room," I say to Thema.

"Okay," she says.

In Thema's room, we put on some Bee Gees and lie down on her bed.

"I'm going to turn it down," she says. "If Mom hears it, she'll come get us to set the table, and there are about forty people here." She lowers the volume, then reaches under her bed. "Look what I got," she says. She holds out a box. Inside, there's sheet music for a whole pile of songs. Thema pulls out the music and reveals a row of Narnia books.

"Where'd you get those?" I ask.

"My cousin in London sent them," she says. Thema is lucky to have a cousin in London to send her stuff. She helps Thema keep up with new music so she can be ready when the time comes to go to London to study. The only books my cousins send are *Archie* comics, which even Gordo can read in an afternoon.

"You can borrow some," says Thema.

Each book is a gem waiting to be cracked open—like a geode. That's what they're called, the gems that you crack open. From the outside they look like normal rocks, but inside they have rows of glistening crystals. Books are like that too. Maybe I can start with *The Silver Chair*. I've read it before, but not for a while. I run my fingers back across the spines and pull *The Silver Chair* out of the box.

"This one?" I ask. Thema nods, but then, with a grin, she pulls three books out of the box to reveal a lower level.

"Look," she says. There are more down there, including some I haven't read before.

"Have you read these yet?" I ask. I long to take one, but I know it isn't fair unless she's already read them. She hands *The Magician's Nephew* to me. It has that new-book smell. I hold it to my nose.

"What are you two doing?" Ebo's voice comes from the doorway. My face flushes. Ebo must think my skin is the most peculiar shade of pink, because I blush every time I see him. I hold the book higher, to hide my face, and wish with all my heart that I'd get over him.

Thema moves over and Ebo sits down beside her on the bed. He hums to the music, then leans over and turns up the volume.

"Don't," says Thema. "We don't want Mom to know we're in here." Ebo laughs and turns the volume up even higher, so the sound bounces off the walls.

"Ebo!" Thema shouts. She throws her pillow at him and beats him with her fists as he backs out of the room, laughing. I turn the volume down, but not before Thema's mom appears in the doorway.

"There you are," she says. "Come help with the table, please." Thema sticks her tongue out at Ebo as we pass him in the hallway.

Mrs. Ampofo leads us to a courtyard behind the pool where there are several tables set up and lots of women bustling around. She hands us each a stack of plates and says, "Put as many on each table as you can," then disappears into one of the neighboring houses.

My pile has yellow plates from Thema's house and red ones that must be from another house in the compound. I place one red, one yellow, one red, one yellow around the table until it's full. I end up with two yellow plates next to each other, so I pick one up again. Some boys run in circles around the table, getting in my way. I swat at them to move.

Mom comes outside with a tray of cutlery and a jug of water.

"What are you doing?" she asks me.

"Red, yellow, red, yellow. It doesn't work," I say.

She hands me the forks and says, "No one will notice tonight."

She's about to turn away, so I say, "Mom, what's going on? Why did Mr. Ampofo invite us here? Dad said the man is in jail, so isn't it all over?"

She doesn't say anything, but the thin line of her lips is an answer in itself.

"Mom?"

"Stop bothering your mother," I hear Dad say. I didn't seen him coming.

"Dad, you tell me, then. What's going on?"

Mom wipes at her eyes, and Dad says, "Leave it, Astrid. We can talk later." He steers Mom away and leaves me standing with a handful of cutlery and no answers. Again.

Ebo and his friends are playing basketball outside the bedrooms. One of them throws the ball at us as we walk back to Thema's room. Thema catches it and runs down the hallway with it in her hands. The boys run after her, shouting, so I back away and look for a quiet place to sit. My head throbs.

The living room is full of adults. Dad and Mom are there, and Mr. Ampofo, and lots of the other people who live in the compound. There isn't enough seating for that many people, so some of the men sit on the floor. Mr. Ampofo is standing near the window, talking, and everyone is listening to him. They all turn and stare at me when I open the door.

Mr. Ampofo stops talking.

"Hi, honey," says Dad. "We're having a meeting. How about you leave us to it?"

"I was looking for somewhere quiet," I say. Some of the men shift in their seats, but no one says anything.

"Dinner will be ready soon," says Dad. "I'll come and find you at the table, okay?" He asks it as a question, but it isn't one, really, so I back out of the room and close the door. My eyes sting. Before today, Dad had never talked to me like that. Like I'm a little kid. But today it seems to be all he's doing.

Ebo's lying on Thema's bed when I get back to her room. There's no sign of anyone else.

"Hi," he says, and for once I don't blush.

"Hi," I say.

"Are you okay?" He sits up and makes room for me on the bed.

I guess my face shows how frustrated I am. I shake my head. "I don't know."

"Let me guess. No one's telling you anything, right?"

"Right," I say. I sit down next to him.

"Welcome to the club," he says.

"They say it's all over, but then they won't tell us anything, and now they're in a meeting, being all secretive."

He nods. It makes me feel better that he's being treated the same way I am.

"Do you think…" My words falter. It's strange talking to Ebo this way, but it's a relief to be my real self with him.

"That we're in danger?" He finishes my sentence.

I nod.

"I don't know," he says. He lies back down and stares at the ceiling.

I watch him breathe in and out, and then I say, "If it gets too dangerous, we can all leave, though, right?"

"Leave?" he says.

"You could go to London. We'd go back home."

Without turning his face, he laughs. "My dad would never leave," he says.

"How come?"

"We're Ghanaian. We'd never leave." He closes his eyes and hums, and I sit at the end of the bed, feeling like a total spaz. I wish that Thema would come in or the earth would swallow me.

Either one, but soon.

TEN

I wait and wait, but over the next few days, no one says anything more about the attempted coup—that's what they call it when someone tries to take over the government. When I ask Dad about it, he looks at me sideways and waves his hand. "Don't worry about it. It's over."

That makes me so mad. He never used to talk to me like that.

"But it could happen again, right? And if it did, what would we do?" I ask.

Dad stands in front of the mirror in his bedroom and combs his hair and straightens his shirt. "It won't happen again, because the man who led the coup is in jail now, so what do you mean, *what would we do*?"

"I mean if it happens again, would we go back home?"

That makes him turn away from the mirror. "Do you want to go home? I thought you liked it here," he says.

There's no point. He isn't listening to me. He hasn't been for a while. Hasn't he seen anything that's going on in this family?

"Mom doesn't."

He sighs and turns back to the mirror. For a minute we both stare into the glass, our eyes catching each other's in the reflection. Then he says, "Don't worry about your mother, Astrid. We all have different ways of coping with things."

"Yeah, hers is to treat us like prisoners," I say.

"Not fair, Astrid. Not fair at all," he says. He puts down his comb and walks out of the room without looking back at me even once. I sit on the edge of their bed and wait until I'm sure I'm not going to cry.

To avoid seeing Dad downstairs, I go outside to wait for Mom to drive us to school.

Thomas is working near the house. "Astrid, help me with this, will you?" he asks. He points to a clump of leaves growing up from the ground.

"There aren't snakes or spiders hiding in there, are there?" I ask.

His whole face laughs, like that's the funniest question anyone ever asked him, and he says, "No, I need to tie them back, that's all."

I wrap the ball of string he hands me around one side of the clump, then reach around so he can take it from me and gather the other side in. As he ties off the string, I say, "Thomas, did you hear about the guy who tried to take over the government last week?"

"I did, Astrid."

"And…" I'm not sure what I want to ask him. There's something strange going on. Dad says the man's in jail, so there's nothing to worry about, but if that's true, then why is everyone being so secretive and serious about it?

Thomas looks up from his knotting and says, "And?"

I shrug. "I'm not sure."

"I'm not sure either," he says.

"But it won't happen again—that's what my dad says."

Thomas nods, then says, "Maybe not."

I want to ask him what he means by *maybe*, but Mom and Gordo come outside, and Mom says, "Hurry, Astrid, we're going to be late," and anyway, Thomas is already reaching around a smaller clump of leaves like he's forgotten we were talking.

We are right behind Sister Mary's scooter at the roadblock, and when she leans toward the soldier something heavy pulls her coat pocket down, and she almost loses her balance. The soldier skips back in alarm, and Sister Mary hurries on. In the parking lot, I try to see what's in her pocket, but it's only when we get to the classroom that I find out Sister Mary has come to school with a snake in her coat pocket. A big snake. With a brother like Gordo, I get my fill of snakes and spiders and stuff. I thought I'd be free of them at school at least.

When Sister Mary pulls the snake out of her pocket and holds it up, I can feel Bassam jump with excitement behind me.

"Figures," I say to Thema, who rolls her eyes.

"Gather round," says Sister Mary, and all of us scrape our chairs back and join her at the back of the classroom where there's a glass terrarium on a table. Sister Mary holds out the snake to each of us, and several people—mostly boys, including Bassam—reach out to pet it, but when the snake head comes toward me, I pull back.

"It's not dangerous," Sister Mary says.

"Still," I say.

"It's dry. Not like you'd expect."

I put my hand out, but as my fingers get close to its head, the snake flicks its tongue, and my fingers flit back to my side. Bassam snickers, but Sister Mary's so focused on her snake, she doesn't notice. I glare at Bassam.

"I don't think Astrid likes snakes," says Bassam.

As usual, my face reddens, but this time Sister Mary says, "Not everyone does," and as soon as she turns away, I stick my tongue out at Bassam.

"Now, we have to build a nest for the snake, so first we need newspaper to shred and some water. Astrid, Thema, you girls go to the headmistress's office and ask for the keys to the storage cabinet."

"Thank you, Sister Mary," I say, and I mean it. A bit of fresh air is what I need.

Out on the breezeway, Thema and I take our time. A wind wafts across the playing fields, and the fresh air feels good.

"Trust Sister Mary to do something like bring a snake to school," says Thema.

"Yeah," I say, but the truth is, even if I don't much like snakes, there's something cool about a woman who drives around with one in her coat pocket.

I giggle and say, "You should have seen the look on the soldier's face at the roadblock. He looked like he thought the snake was about to bite him!"

Thema and I are still laughing when the door opens and the headmistress walks out of her office.

"Girls," she says.

"Good morning, Miss," we chant, trying to hide our laughter.

"Did Sister Mary send you?"

"We're to ask for the key to the storage cabinet," Thema says.

"Is this for the snake?"

"Yes, Miss," I say.

"All right, come in." She walks back into her office and beckons for me and Thema to follow. I've never been in her office before, and I can tell by how closely Thema crowds behind me that she's as nervous as I am.

The phone rings, which startles all of us, since the phones seldom work, and we stare at it for a minute before the headmistress says, "Excuse me for a moment, please" and picks up the receiver. She waves at two seats, and Thema and I sit down.

It seems rude to listen to her on the phone, so Thema and I both lean in to the radio that sits on a small table between the two chairs. As we listen, the music is interrupted by a man's voice. He speaks in Twi, so I have to ask Thema, "What's he saying?"

"Jerry Rawlings' trial will be broadcast on this station," Thema says. "He's the man who led the coup."

Miss covers the phone receiver with her hand and listens too. When the man's done and the music comes back on, she shakes her head before she says goodbye to the caller and hangs up.

"What do you think it means?" asks Thema.

"It means this is not over yet," says Miss. She stands up and walks to the window. Her answer is not a surprise to me. Something in the way my dad and Thema's dad have been talking makes me think they don't believe it's over either, even if they keep saying it is.

"Miss?"

"Yes, Astrid."

I'm not sure what I want to ask, so I say, "Could it happen again? I mean, could someone else try to take over the government?"

Miss sits down again. She stares out the window and I think she's not going to answer, but then she says, "It could happen."

"How come, Miss?"

"Because life has been hard for Ghanaians for a long time now. Many people are looking for something new. They want to be able to buy food in the stores and have good job opportunities for their kids and be able to live in nice houses."

"My dad says Rawlings's timing is bad because of the elections coming up," I say.

"You can't expect everyone to agree, Astrid."

"What do you think, Miss?" asks Thema.

"I agree with Astrid's father about the timing. I don't know why anyone would want to interrupt things now." She reaches into a drawer in her desk, then stands up and hands the key to me.

I'm quiet as I take it from her, but when she says, "What is it, Astrid?" I say, "I hope it doesn't happen. I mean, I hope no one else tries to have a coup." My voice is small, because I realize as I speak that this is what has been sitting in the back of my brain. This is why no one is telling us anything. They're scared it will happen again.

Again, Miss stares out the window like she hasn't heard me. Then she says, "It's a mistake to broadcast this trial. I won't be too surprised if there is some unrest after that."

"What do you mean, *unrest*?"

She shakes her head. "I'm not sure what I mean. These are uncertain times for Ghana. Let's hope I'm mistaken and the elections go ahead as planned." She opens the office door and motions for me and Thema to leave.

"Thank you, Miss," I say as Thema and I walk past her.

"You're welcome, girls," she says.

Out in the breezeway, Thema says, "She's nicer than I thought."

I nod. She is nicer than I expected, and she's the only person who's taken me seriously. But she hasn't put my mind at ease at all. Not at all.

ELEVEN

The house is in an uproar when we get home from school. Mom hardly glances at us when we walk into the house. She's in the living room searching for something. The strap of her tank top has fallen across her arm, and her hair's coming loose from its elastic.

"What's going on?" I ask.

"I can't find Piper," she says. She moves so fast, her voice trails her. The living room looks like dogs have been fighting in it. Furniture is turned over. Cushions are on the floor. She's even managed to move the big potted palm from its corner. There's a strong smell of earth in the room from some of it spilling out of the pot.

"Mom, calm down. She's probably fallen asleep somewhere. It's so hot. Have you looked in her room?"

I speak slowly. I thought she was getting better. Seeing her like this again is scary.

"I've looked everywhere," she says, and this time her words are more like sobs. This isn't just Mom panicking because she hasn't seen Piper for a few minutes. Her eyes are red, her mouth, a tight line. My chest constricts and I have to take a deep breath before I say, "Mom, slow down. Where have you looked? Have you tried the yard?"

"I've looked everywhere," she says as she tugs at the curtains.

"Mom, Mom, slow down. She's not hiding behind the curtains. Tell me where you've looked." I try to sound calm, but the scent of her panic is sharp, and it makes my voice catch. She doesn't slow down, and she doesn't answer, and it hits me that Piper might really be missing.

"Gordo and I will help," I say. Gordo hasn't said anything, but his face is white, and he's shaking.

"It's okay, Gordo, we'll find her," I say. He nods, but I can tell he's biting back tears. He slides his hand into mine, and his palm is slick with sweat. That freaks me out. Gordo the daredevil is scared. The possibilities flood into me, and I too feel tears bombard my eyes.

"Go check the yard," I say to Gordo, mostly to get him away from Mom's panic. He stares at me with wide eyes, but then lets go of my hand and rushes out the door. I follow him outside. Somewhere through my fear the thought comes that if Piper's in the house, she's probably okay, so I'll let Mom look there. If she's outside... I don't want to finish that thought. Suddenly all the dangers Mom's always going on about seem real, and I imagine spiders and biting ants and cobras and pythons and murderous germs everywhere.

Thomas is washing the car, but he stops when Gordo and I run out of the house.

"What's the matter?" asks Thomas.

"Piper's missing," I say.

He creases his forehead. "What do you mean?"

"What do you mean, *what do you mean*?"

"Abena took her shopping. They're down the street. Your mother didn't tell you?" says Thomas.

The relief floods over me. "Oh," I say.

Gordo flushes red, then laughs a crazy-edged laugh. "I'll go tell Mom," he says. He's about to run into the house, but Thomas says, "Your mom already knows."

"She does?" I say. The flooding of relief in my veins is replaced by something else. Something prickly. Fear. Gordo looks at me with big eyes.

"She must. I'm sure Abena told her," says Thomas.

"Oh," I say again. Maybe Abena didn't tell her. Maybe Mom hasn't totally lost her marbles. Maybe she really doesn't know where Piper is.

"Gordo, you go in and tell Mom, and I'll run down and get Abena and Piper," I say, and then I dash down the drive.

Abena isn't far down the street, so when I call, "Abena, Abena," she waves and points me out to Piper, who grins broadly and waves too. My heart bounces in my chest at the sight of Piper happily waving.

She's okay.

Really okay.

I'm hardly halfway to them when Mom tears past me, with Gordo close behind. The three of us race to Piper, and when Mom gets there she grabs Piper right out of Abena's arms and hugs her so tightly that Piper cries.

"Don't ever do that again," Mom says to Abena. Her voice has a roughness I've never heard.

Abena says, "What did I do, Mrs. Johnson?"

"What did you do? You took off with Piper and I didn't know where she was. Anything could have happened to her. She could have been stung by something or fallen into a ditch or been swallowed by a snake or kidnapped or who knows what!" Mom's voice is hoarse.

Abena looks shaky, and she says, "Mrs. Johnson, I thought you knew she was with me."

"Well, I didn't." Mom stares at Abena, and Gordo and I stand together and hold our breath.

"I'm sorry, Mrs. Johnson, I did tell you," says Abena, looking at the ground.

"My husband will hear about this," says Mom, and she spins around and walks back to the house with Piper. Gordo and I don't move. It's like we're stuck to the ground, and we don't know what to do until Abena picks up a basket lying at her feet and places it on her head, then slowly walks back to the house. Gordo slips his hand into mine. His fingers are cold. I grasp them tightly and we follow Abena.

That evening after dinner, when I'm supposed to be in my room doing homework, I walk down the stairs to get a glass of water from the fridge and overhear Mom and Dad talking to Abena. I can't hear what they're saying, but I can tell their voices are raised. Just as I'm about to turn around and go back upstairs, Abena walks out of the kitchen. She's crying. I run into the stairwell and hold my breath until she passes.

I feel like I've been punched in the face. I'm not sure if I feel worse for Abena, for being yelled at for something she didn't do, or for Mom, for being so upset about something that didn't happen.

Mom and Dad come out of the kitchen a second later. I stay still because I hear Dad saying, "We'll keep the kids close, Joanne. I won't let anything happen to them."

"Can you promise that?" Mom says.

There's silence, and then Dad sighs. "Of course not, Joanne. But…" He doesn't finish.

"I don't want them going anywhere. Anywhere at all. At least here we have walls and a phone—some of the time," Mom says.

"Joanne, the man's in jail. What can he do?" asks Dad.

Mom storms away, leaving me and Dad standing on opposite sides of a wall.

TWELVE

Dad drives me and Gordo and Piper to Thema's house on Sunday morning.

"Aren't we going to the beach?" asks Gordo. Sunday is our usual beach day.

"Not today."

When Gordo starts to object, Dad snaps, "Not today, Gordo."

"Shut up, Gordo," I say. Gordo's too young to understand, but I know Dad is trying to let Mom have some time to calm down after what happened on Friday. Yesterday he made us both be quiet all day, and today he's getting us even more out of her way.

There are four parcels on the kitchen table at Thema's house when we walk in. Thema hovers around them, and as soon as we come into the room, she says, "Mine," picking one up and shaking it softly next to her ear.

"What are they?" I ask.

"Packages from Aunt Louise in London," she says.

"More?" I ask. I sure wish Aunt Alice would send packages like she said she would.

Thema unwraps the parcel slowly, like she wants to savor each moment. She picks off the tape and unbinds the string, then folds back the brown paper. I want to reach out and tear it away, so I sit on my hands to keep them still. When she finally gets the cardboard box open, we both lean forward to see what's inside.

"Books!" I say. I can't help myself. I reach into the box and slide the books over so I can read the titles. "Thema, look—she sent it."

"Yay," she says, and she pulls *The Last Battle* out of the box. It's the final one in the Chronicles of Narnia series, and both Thema and I are dying to read it. There are also sheets of music, including a whole book of Donna Summer songs.

Ebo comes into the room and says, "Hey, what did she send me?" He grabs his box and tears off the string and paper. Inside are two polo shirts, five chocolate bars and some books on soccer and animals.

"Cool," says Ebo, holding up the chocolate.

"Oh, did she send some for me?" asks Thema. She digs around in her box, but apart from the books and sheet music, there's only a blouse and a skirt, both of which she pushes aside. "No chocolate," she says, disappointed.

Ebo unwraps one of his chocolate bars. It has melted a bit in the heat but still looks delicious. He breaks it into pieces. "What will you do for me if I give you some?" he asks.

"Give me a piece," Thema says.

"What will you do?"

"I don't have to do anything. Give me one piece." She puts out her hand, but Ebo raises the chocolate above his head, where she can't reach it.

"Ebo…I'll tell Mom." Thema's voice is almost whining, she wants that chocolate so much.

Ebo pops a piece into his mouth. "Ummm…" he says, and he smacks his lips.

"Mom," yells Thema.

Ebo laughs and offers us both a piece of chocolate.

"No thanks," I say, but he says, "Oh go on. I was always going to give you some. I just like to tease Thema."

The chocolate is rich and creamy. I can't remember the last time I ate some, and it's like nothing I've ever tasted.

"This is delicious," I say.

"Of course. It's made with Ghanaian cocoa beans," says Ebo.

"Do you want to borrow a book?" Thema asks me.

"Can I?" Something new to read! I want *The Last Battle*, but I know Thema hasn't read it yet, so instead I choose *Watership Down*. I've heard it's good.

"You can read *The Last Battle* as soon as I'm done," says Thema.

Thema's mom comes in and opens her package. It's full of boring stuff like Band-Aids and toothpaste, but she smiles and laughs at everything she opens, and she seems as happy with her box as Thema and Ebo are with theirs. It makes me wonder what Mom would want in a package if Aunt Alice ever got around to sending one. I know what I want. Books and tapes. Gordo wants more marbles and toy soldiers and *Archie* comics, and Piper would be happy with anything. Dad grumbles about not getting newspapers until they're out of date, but Mom never talks about what she misses.

Ebo and Gordo go off to Ebo's room to poke at a spider Ebo has found. Even though Ebo's fifteen and Gordo's only ten, they really get along. It's because they both like to stare and prod at insects and other gross stuff. Thema and I get as far away from them as we can when they're doing that. Today we have Piper with us, so Thema and I take her outside and sit under a tree. I scan the area for anthills and other possible dangers before I let her down on the ground.

"Let's make her a swing," says Thema.

"Out of what?"

"How about an old tire?" says Thema. "Or a plank of wood."

It's a great idea, and I make a mental note to remember to ask Thomas for something to make a swing out of at home.

"Let's ask Kofi for help," says Thema, and she skips off across the courtyard to find their gardener. Piper and I follow more slowly, and we find Thema already explaining to Kofi what she wants. She speaks in Twi, but I can tell what she's saying by her gestures. Kofi smiles and pats Piper's head and strokes her cheek. She giggles, as usual, and Kofi's smile grows even bigger.

"I have a better idea," says Kofi in English. "Follow me."

He leads us behind the houses to where the washtubs and drying racks are. At the back, by the garden wall, there's a heap of stuff. He pushes aside badminton rackets, a volleyball net and some cricket bats and pulls out a rope hammock.

"Perfect!" I say.

"How will we hang it?" asks Thema as she takes it from him.

Kofi scrounges around until he finds two coils of rope. "Tie each end to a tree," he says. "Carefully," he adds.

I pick Piper up, and Thema and I run back to the side of the house. The ropes are old and frayed in places, but we manage to get them around two tree trunks, and we sling the hammock between them.

"Want to go for a swing, Piper?" Thema asks.

"Wait," I say. I'm not sure of the rope, so I want to try it first. I lean into the hammock and push. The hammock swings a bit but doesn't fall, so I lower myself into it and lay back. It swings wildly, and my head tips toward the ground.

"Whoa!" I say as I straighten myself. "I think we'd better loosen it so it doesn't swing that much. And we should lower it too, so that even if she does fall out, she won't have far to go."

Thema laughs. "Okay, Mrs. Hammock Police."

I laugh too, but I make her untie one end while I untie the other, and we lower the ropes until they're about three feet off the ground.

"Maybe we can bring out a pillow to put on the ground. Just in case," I say.

Thema says, "You sound like your mom."

My hands freeze in mid-knot. Even though Thema is smiling, she's also shaking her head like I'm acting crazy. Am I being like Mom?

"I'm trying to keep her safe," I say. "She's only two."

"I know. But she won't hurt herself if she falls two feet," says Thema. She's right. Babies fall all the time. As long as the hammock isn't moving too much, Piper will be fine.

I test the ropes again to make sure the knots are good, then say, "Piper, do you want to try the hammock?"

It's low enough that she can reach it, and she tries to climb in by herself, but Thema picks her up and sets her down safely in the middle. Then I stand behind Piper's back and push. Piper squeals and laughs and claps her hands.

"I guess she likes it," Thema says.

"I guess she does."

It's shady under the trees, and Thema and I take turns pushing Piper or sitting in front of her and catching her toes, which makes her laugh.

After a while, Thema's mom comes out with three glasses of lemonade.

"Look what we made for Piper, Mom," says Thema.

"Oh, look at that," she says with a laugh. "It's perfect. We should have put that back up years ago." She takes Thema's place playing with Piper's toes, and Thema and I sip our drinks. Piper laughs and squeals, and Mrs. Ampofo laughs with her.

When Piper's had enough, she squirms, and I help her out of the hammock. She scrambles to the ground and climbs into my lap. She wants to drink some of my lemonade, so I hold the glass for her while she has some.

"You're such a good big sister, Astrid," says Thema's mom. "I bet your mom is really proud of you."

It's all I can do not to cry when she says that. I try to smile at her, but I have to look down at Piper instead. I stroke her hair and say, "I try to be a good sister, but it doesn't always work."

Mrs. Ampofo nods and sips her lemonade. "Life isn't always predictable, but you do your best," she says.

She's right. I do.

THIRTEEN

Over the next week, it's so hot that Gordo and I beg Mom to let us go swimming at Thema's pool, but she shakes her head every time we ask and says, "It's too dangerous to be out on the roads." When I ask if that means we shouldn't go to school, she stares at me with an evil eye that Sister Mary would be proud of and says, "Watch it, young lady."

It's no better on the weekend, when Dad's at home. On Sunday morning Gordo and I get ourselves ready to go to the beach, but when we come downstairs, Dad just shakes his head and says, "Find something to do at home today."

"Aww," whines Gordo, and he flings himself into a chair. I feel like doing the same, but I know it will be no use. At least I have a new book to read. The power's been off for days, so I sit outside under the tree and read

Watership Down until the rain starts and I have to go to my hot, sweaty room. Some days that room feels like a prison.

On Monday I wake early. The power is still off, and I'm sweaty and worn out from sleeping poorly. I get up and go downstairs and out to the front yard. The sun isn't properly up yet, but the roosters are crowing, and a surprising number of people walk past on the street. The air isn't exactly cool, but it's better than inside, so I sit down on the step to listen to the sounds of early morning.

I'm drifting back to sleep when I hear voices at the gate, and Thomas steps into view. He waves goodbye to someone and walks up the drive.

"Asteroid," he calls. "What are you doing up?"

I stand and stretch. "I couldn't sleep. It was too hot."

"Hot?" He laughs. He's wearing a windbreaker and toque, and I'm in my T-shirt and shorts. We'll never agree on what hot and cold feel like.

"How come you're here so early?" I ask. We walk around to the little shed on the side of the house where we keep the garden tools, and Thomas unlocks the padlock. "This is my normal time," he says as he takes off his jacket and toque and hangs them in the shed.

"So you *are* warm," I say to tease him.

"I am now." He pulls out a rake and a shovel and takes his shortwave radio off the shelf, then shoos me out of the shed so he can lock it up again. I haven't ever thought about it before, but Thomas is always here when Gordo and I come down for breakfast in the mornings. I've often seen him doing something in the garden. I guess he leaves his house early so he can work before it gets too hot.

As we walk toward the kitchen, he fiddles with the dial on the radio; it wails and shrieks in the still air. A voice wavers and then grows stronger as Thomas gets the station tuned in.

A deep voice booms out, and Thomas stands straighter and holds up the radio.

"Who was that? What was he talking about?" I ask.

"That was Rawlings speaking at his court-martial," he says. He puts down his rake and shovel to take the cup of tea Abena hands him through the kitchen door.

"Did you hear that?" he asks her. There's a challenge in his voice.

Abena says, "That stuff he's saying about corruption. What's he going to do about it? It's everywhere." She scowls and blows into her tea mug. Steam clouds her glasses. I glance from one to the other of them, one so happy, the other not impressed at all.

"That's what Rawlings wants to fix," says Thomas. "He wants to get rid of the hoarders. You heard him." His face glows, but Abena keeps scowling.

"What are hoarders?" I ask.

"Nothing you have to worry about," Abena says, but Thomas says, "Rich people who buy up stuff in the stores, then sell it from their homes at higher prices. But that Rawlings, he's going to get rid of them. He's going to—"

Abena interrupts him. "He's in jail. He's not going to do anything."

It seems like Thomas is in too good a mood to let Abena get him down, because he says, "You wait."

"Why are you so happy?" Abena asks.

"Because Esi got a big order the other day for more animals, and Rawlings is going to set things straight, and it's a cool day and we might get rain."

"Hmmm," says Abena and slams the kitchen door.

"She's never happy," I say to make Thomas feel better, but he laughs and says, "She doesn't bother me."

"I'm glad you got an order for more animals," I say. I can picture Thomas and Esi walking around their neighborhood, looking at houses they want to buy. I can see them sitting under a big tree, sipping tea and playing with the baby they'll have once they get their own home.

Thomas grins. "Someday I'll make animals full-time. I'll import wood from all over the world and make them out of teak and cedar and purpleheart."

I've never heard of purpleheart, but I know that a lot of cedar grows back home in British Columbia. "When I go home, I'll send you some cedar. The best I can find," I say.

Thomas gives me a high five, and I go back inside to get ready for school.

By the time I come back down in my uniform, everyone's up and the house has lost its morning calm. Piper tosses her grapefruit on the floor and makes a sour face, and Dad runs around shouting about his wallet, and Mom lectures Gordo about eating more before he goes to school. Strangely, the only one who doesn't say anything is Gordo. He sits at the table for a while, then pushes his grapefruit away and goes upstairs.

"What's up with him?" Mom asks.

I shrug. Gordo's Gordo—that's what's up with him.

In school Sister Mary's talking about Ghanaian history again. She talks a lot about Ghanaian history. This time it's about how the Portuguese sailed along this coast in the 1400s. They were looking for gold and ivory and pepper and slaves. I know Sister Mary wants us to understand why Ghana is the Black Star of Africa, and why the elections are so important, but I really wish she'd get to the point and not spend so much time talking about it.

Now she's talking about how the Portuguese went as far inland as Ouagadougou. I catch Thema's eye when Sister Mary says the word *Ouagadougou*, and we both laugh out loud.

"Astrid, stand up and tell the class what's so funny."

I can't. I really can't say anything at all, because the laughter is coming up my nose and out my eyes and if I try to speak I'll explode, so I shake my head.

"Thema?" Sister Mary says.

Thema stands slowly but stares at the floor. Thema hates getting into trouble, and when a tear falls down her cheek, I know it's not the laughter making her eyes water.

I swallow hard and stand. "Sister Mary?"

"Astrid."

"We're sorry. We were laughing about how funny the word *Ouagadougou* sounds. We're sorry." My laughter's gone now, because I hate seeing Thema cry.

Sister Mary considers me and Thema, standing side by side, our heads hanging.

"Thank you for being honest," she says, and I'm about to slide back into my seat when she adds, "You two can sit outside until the end of the period."

Something rises in my throat and almost chokes me. I splutter, but Thema grabs my arm and pulls me outside before I can say anything. I sigh and slump back against the rail.

Somehow, everything I do in school gets me in trouble. I can't seem to get it right.

"Sister Mary hates me," I say.

"No she doesn't," says Thema.

"Yes she does."

Thema sits down next to me so that we're both leaning against the rail. She wipes her eyes and slings her arm across my shoulder. A breeze stirs the red dirt at our feet, and the tamarind pods rustle in the tree across the compound. A goat bleats from somewhere nearby. Thema and I sit together in silence.

Life's not fair sometimes.

When the period's over and break begins, Sister Mary opens the classroom door and kids stream out. As he walks past me, Bassam thrusts a piece of paper into my hand.

"What's this?" I ask, but he runs down the stairs without answering. Thema has a paper too, so we open them together. *You are invited to a party*, they say.

"Bassam's invited us to a party?" I ask.

"Look at your face," says Thema with a laugh. "You look like you saw a cow fly."

"Well…" I'm surprised. Bassam tortures me every day. I can't believe he wants me to come to a party.

"He invited the whole class. He does it every year, and his house is amazing, so you have to come," says Harpreet, plunking down next to us.

I bunch the paper in my hand and throw it into the trashcan.

"What are you doing?" Thema asks.

"There's no point. Mom will never let me go."

Thema reaches into the trash and pulls out the paper. She smooths it out and hands it back to me. "You never know," she says.

I bunch it back up and toss it away again. "Yes, I do." And I do. Mom will never let me go. The only places she ever lets us go these days are school and Thema's house, and that's only because Dad makes her.

"No, you don't," says Harpreet. She fishes the paper out and hands it to me. I take it and shove it into my pocket. I know she won't, but it's not worth getting into a flip about.

Mom lets Thema come over on Sunday afternoon after her family gets back from the beach.

We have a snack, then head outside. It's so hot, all we have energy for is sitting around under the tree, listening to the chickens next door. There isn't a cloud in the sky, and the heat makes a haze over everything.

Gordo wanders outside and sits in the grass with us. He moves slowly.

"Where are your friends?" I ask. I'm really telling him to bug off, but he doesn't seem to get the hint, because he says, "I sent them away" and then slides down into the little hammock Thomas slung for Piper after I told him about the one we made at Thema's house. It's too small for Gordo, but he stays in it anyway.

He stares at the sky and rocks slowly.

"Gordo, go ask Abena for some lemonade," I say, but he doesn't move.

"Gordo," I say again.

He stares at me but doesn't say anything, so I say, "Are you okay?"

"I don't feel good," he says.

I lean over and touch Gordo's forehead. It's hot, so I put my hand on Thema's to compare. She's hot too, so it's hard to tell if Gordo's head is warmer than it should be. It's so stinking hot, we all feel like we're burning up. "Do you have a fever?" I ask.

Gordo doesn't answer except to close his eyes.

"Maybe we should go get your mom," says Thema.

"No. I'll get him some lemonade," I say. Mom's in the house having a nap with Piper. I could go and get her, but the thought of that makes me feel like lead.

When I come back with a glass of lemonade for Gordo, he's fallen asleep, so I leave the glass next to the hammock and walk to the front of the house with Thema to wait for her mom to pick her up.

After Thema leaves, I go back to Gordo to see if he's drunk his lemonade. He's still asleep. The lemonade was never cold, because of the power being out, and now it's full of ants. I tip the liquid onto the grass and watch the ants swim away. Gordo's forehead is definitely hotter than it should be now, and his face is dry and flushed.

His breathing is even but heavy. I know I should go and tell Mom. I know I should, but instead I sit on the ground next to him and push the hammock so it sways. Gordo groans and stirs but doesn't wake up.

I touch his forehead again, and this time I have no doubt. He's got a fever.

I draw in a long breath and focus.

"I'm going to run you a bath," I say to Gordo. Piper's had fevers hundreds of times, and Mom always runs a cool bath and sponges her down in it. Maybe if I can get Gordo's fever down, he'll feel better and we won't have to tell Mom.

"Come on, Gordo, wake up," I say.

I reach into the hammock and pull on his arms until he opens his eyes and says, "Stop it. What are you doing?"

"You're having a bath," I say.

"I don't want a bath."

"You're having one anyway,"

"You sound like Mom," he says, pulling his arms out of my grasp and snuggling back into the hammock.

It's true. I sound like Mom. That thought makes me try even harder.

"Come on," I say again. This time I push the hammock over so that Gordo almost tips, and he grumbles as he gets out of it. I push him into the house and up the stairs. He moans, but I say, "Shhh. The baby's sleeping," and he quietens.

When we reach the bathroom, I turn on the tap and pray that water comes out. It does. At first it's brown, but after it runs for a few minutes, it turns clear, and I put the stopper in the tub and say, "Climb in, Gordo."

He sits on the edge of the bathtub and refuses to move, so I take a cloth from the cupboard and soak it in the bathwater, then squeeze it over Gordo's head. The water slides around his ears and down his nose.

"That feels good," he says, so I do it again, this time rubbing the cool water into his neck as well.

"Come on, get into the bath," I say, but he still doesn't move, so I pull off his sandals and tug at his shirt.

"Leave me alone," he whines.

"Come on, Gordo."

"Stop it." He shoves me, and I stumble into the cupboard, slamming the door. We both jump at the sound, and I say, "Gordo, you'll wake up Mom!"

"Stop it," he says as I pull at his shirt again.

"What's going on?" Mom is standing in the doorway.

Gordo and I both freeze, and then he slumps against the wall and closes his eyes.

"Gordo!" Mom leaps to his side and cradles him. "Astrid, what's going on?"

"Gordo's sick. I mean, he has a fever, and I'm trying to sponge him off. He won't get into the bathtub."

Mom rubs her hand over his forehead. "Oh my god, Astrid, he's burning up. How long has he been like this?

Why didn't you call me?" Her voice is shrill and her hands are frantic as she pulls off his T-shirt and yanks off his shorts. Gordo doesn't resist. He lets her lift him into the bathtub and pour water over his shoulders and back. Mom mumbles something to him, and he leans into her shoulder.

"Mom, is there anything I can do?" I ask. She doesn't turn her head as she says, "Go and phone your father, Astrid. I think you've done enough already."

It's not the words she says that make my limbs turn to concrete. It's the way her hands move so fast, and how she clasps Gordo to her chest like she's rescued him from dying.

FOURTEEN

The next morning I pull on my T-shirt and shorts and a light cotton sweater and tiptoe past Gordo's room. I'm careful not to wake anyone, since Mom and Dad were up most of the night with Gordo. I know because I heard them walking up and down the hall.

The yard is empty, so I settle down to listen to the wind in the trees and the roosters next door, and to smell the scent of the jasmine. Thomas told me once that flowers throw their scent in the early morning. I didn't know what he meant then, but I do now, because at this time of day the smell hits me as soon as I open the door.

When Thomas arrives, he laughs at me. "We'll make a Ghanaian of you yet," he says, pointing at my sweater.

There are clouds in the sky. They glower over the sun and bring the temperature down a bit.

As usual, Thomas walks to the side of the house, unlocks the tool shed, takes off his toque and jacket, and gathers his rake and shovel and radio before heading to the kitchen door to ask Abena for a cup of tea. He fiddles with the radio dial until the station comes in clearly, and when it does, he stops and turns up the volume.

"*The ranks have just got me out of my cell. In other words, the ranks have just taken over the destiny of this country.*"

"Who's that?" I ask, but Thomas puts his hand up to silence me.

"*Fellow officers, if we are to avoid any bloodshed, I plead with you not to attempt to stand in their way because they are full of malice. Hatred—hatred we have forced into them through all these years of suppression.*"

The voice stops and the radio goes to static.

"Yes," shouts Thomas, and he kicks his foot into the air karate-style.

"What?" I ask.

"Rawlings! His men have released him from jail. He's taken over the government. Yes!" Thomas's face shines with excitement.

I'm confused. How can this be? Wasn't he in jail, waiting to be executed for trying to take over the government?

Thomas laughs and gives the frangipani leaves high fives.

Abena opens the door and comes out smiling. She and Thomas hug each other and smile and she cries and they hug some more. Then they both laugh.

It's strange to see Thomas and Abena like this. I thought Abena would be mad that Rawlings has taken over the government, but she doesn't seem to be. Then I remember the evening we spent at Thema's house the first time Rawlings tried to take over the government, and how serious all the adults were. I bite my lip.

What does this mean? Dad didn't seem happy then.

The day seems darker, even though Thomas and Abena are laughing and dancing around each other. I leave them to go and find Dad. I need to talk to him.

As I enter the kitchen, Mom walks in and says, "You're not going to school this morning." I stop and consider what she's said. The darkness of the day seems even heavier, because if we're not going to school, it means she thinks we're in danger. Then again…this is Mom.

"Gordo's sick, and I need you to take care of Piper," she says as she opens the fridge door and looks in.

So this has nothing to do with Rawlings being released from jail and taking over the government.

She closes the fridge door without taking anything out and marches out of the kitchen.

"Wait, Mom," I call as I run to catch up with her. "Where's Dad?" But she doesn't even slow her stride and takes the stairs two at a time. She almost runs down the hall and into Gordo's room. Dad's there already. He's dressed for work, but he looks rumpled. He sits on the edge of Gordo's bed and strokes Gordo's forehead. He looks at Gordo like he wants to cry but is somehow keeping his eyes from knowing what his brain is thinking. He whispers something to Gordo that I can't hear.

Dad stands and lets Mom sit down, then leans across her to stroke Gordo's forehead one more time.

"I'll be as quick as I can," he says to Mom. She doesn't move as he leaves the room.

"Dad," I say as he walks past me.

"What?"

"Rawlings—" I say, but Dad puts his finger on his lips and pulls me out of the room.

"I know, Astrid." He stares back into Gordo's room as I wait for him to say something else, but he just shrugs and says, "I'll be back as soon as I can. Don't worry. Everything will be fine."

I remember how frightened Mom looked the last time I heard Dad say those words, and now I understand, because I don't believe him.

Not at all.

"Dad," I say, but he's not listening. He pats me on the head like I'm a little kid and strides away.

I spend the rest of the day watching Piper and listening to the radio with Thomas. Whenever he comes back to the hammock, where Piper and I sit, I ask him, "What's happening now?"

"They've captured General Akuffo," he says the first time.

"They've taken over Broadcast House," he says the next time.

"They're calling on the soldiers to keep calm," he says the third time.

"Are you sure?" I ask. It all seems like it's taking place in a different country, because at the end of the driveway, goats still graze and people walk past like nothing's is happening.

"They say it's crazy downtown," says Thomas.

"Oh," I say. Dad's office is downtown. He must have driven right past all the soldiers. The darkness of the day closes in.

I pick up Piper and go inside to see if maybe Dad's phoned to say he's okay. Mom's still in Gordo's room, sitting in the same place she was when I last saw her.

"Hi, Mom," I say, but she puts her finger on her lips and points to Gordo, who's sleeping. I sit next to her and pass Piper over, but she doesn't take Piper from me. Instead, she leans over and strokes Gordo's face.

Piper crawls to the floor to play with Gordo's toy soldiers, but I scoop her up again before she does something dangerous like put one in her mouth. Mom doesn't say anything.

"Did Dad call?" I ask.

"No. Why?" she says.

I open my mouth to tell her about Rawlings and what's happened, then close it again. She's so distracted by Gordo, she wouldn't hear me anyway.

"Get me a cool cloth. Quick," she says, and she leans over and fusses with his sheet.

"Mom," I say.

"Quick," she says, so I take Piper and run to the bathroom, where I pour cold water onto a cloth.

"Is this tap water?" she asks when I hand it to her, and she thrusts it back at me when I nod. "There's some water Abena boiled in a bowl in the hallway. Use that," she says.

My eyes blur as I take a clean cloth from the pile in the hallway and soak it in the bowl of water.

I take the cloth back to her and say, "Piper and I will be downstairs if you need us" as I leave the room.

Later in the afternoon when a car comes into the driveway, I rush outside, but it's not Dad. Thomas is there, and the man driving the car says something to him in Twi that I don't understand.

"Astrid, this is Peter. Your dad sent him to take me and Abena home," Thomas says. "Will you get Abena?"

"But why?" I ask.

Peter seems impatient to go, and he's already getting back into the driver's seat, but Thomas says, "Remember I said they were calling on the soldiers to keep calm?"

I nod.

"Some of them are not listening. There's been some shooting in town, and your dad thinks we may have trouble getting home, so he sent a car to make sure we get across the city safely. It was very kind of him."

My breath comes sharply, but Thomas says, "It's okay, Asteroid. We know the back ways—we'll be fine."

"Do you have to go?" I ask. I don't want to be left alone with Mom and Gordo.

Thomas walks around the car and puts his arm across my shoulder, "Astrid, you will be fine here. Everything will be fine. But I have to go and make sure Esi's okay. Do you understand?"

"Yes," I say. I understand. I do. But as Abena gets ready to leave, and as she and Thomas drive away, I wrap my arms around myself and try not to shiver.

Piper's a heavy burden today, so I take her to the living room, where she can play on the floor and I won't have to worry about her. She plays with the blocks no one remembered to put away, and I sit on the sofa and stare out the window. Every time I hear a car drive past, I start, and it seems like hours before Dad's car finally turns into the driveway. I scoop up Piper and run outside so fast, we collide with Dad as he opens the door.

"Whoa," he says as we right ourselves.

"Dad." I want to say his name and hug him, and I don't care that my voice catches and I start to cry. Dad puts his arms around me and Piper and squeezes, and we stay that way until Piper squirms to be released.

"How's Gordo?" he asks when we let go.

"Not…" I'm still crying and my voice squeaks, so I try again. "Not good."

"And your mom?"

I shake my head.

Dad frowns. "The car came for Thomas and Abena?"

"Yes."

"Good," he says, and I want to say, *No, not good, because I've been alone all afternoon waiting for you and because I don't know who to worry about more, you or Gordo or Mom.*

Dad hugs me again, and I say, "What was it like?" instead.

"Fine. It was okay. Things are under control. I spent most of the day making sure all the staff were safe.

And now I should go inside and check on Gordo and your mom." He squares his shoulders like he's bracing himself. "What have you told her?" he asks.

"Nothing," I say.

Dad puts his hand on my shoulder. "It's been a hard day, hasn't it, Astrid?"

I nod, because I can't talk.

"I think...I think we won't tell her yet that there's been a coup. That Rawlings was successful this time. We'll let her focus on Gordo for now," he says.

He smiles at me then and takes my hand. "Let's go check on them, okay?"

Together, we walk up the stairs. I'm glad he's home safe, and I'm happy we're holding hands and walking together, but I can't understand why Mom gets to be the person with only one thing to worry about.

FIFTEEN

Gordo's worse in the morning. Mom hasn't moved from his bedside for at least twenty-four hours. Twice in the night I woke up and heard her voice in Gordo's room. The first time, she was singing. The second time, she was crying. Now she sits there mopping his forehead with a cool cloth and feeding him Aspirin and saying over and over, "We should never have come. Look at what's happened, Richard. We should never have come."

Dad stands in the doorway, chewing his lip. Every time Mom says that, he shrinks a little.

I nose my head under Dad's elbow and wrap my arms around him. I'm so tired and hot, my fingers and toes feel like sausages. Dad's slippery with sweat, and it stinks on him, but it's comforting to lay my head against his chest, so I stay there.

Gordo groans, and Mom whimpers and smooths his forehead again. "Richard, you have to take him," she says.

"Joanne, the streets are not safe. I've told you that. Besides, who knows if the clinic is even open?" he says.

Mom sits up straight and looks Dad right in the eye. They stare at each other like they're having a battle, and then she says, "If he dies, Richard, it will be your fault."

Both Dad and I gasp and stiffen. He pulls away from me and walks down the hallway. When he reaches his room, he slams the door. He's gone to change—I know it. He's going to take Gordo to the clinic, and it will be Mom's fault if something happens to them.

It will be Mom's fault.

I stand paralyzed in the doorway, staring at Mom. My face reddens slowly as her words sink in, but her eyes are blank. It's like I'm not there at all. It's like she's not there either. She turns away from me and bends down to Gordo again.

I don't think. I run to my room and grab the first T-shirt I see lying on the floor, then pull on a pair of underwear and some shorts. I'm back in the hallway before Dad is. He comes out of his room fully dressed and marches to Gordo's room. He scoops Gordo out of bed and carries him across the room. I follow him down the stairs, out the front door and to the car. I open the car door and help him settle Gordo in the back seat, but Gordo's too sick to sit up and slumps over, and we can't get his seat belt on. Dad stands and runs his hands through his hair. The sound he makes is like a dog growling. I slide into the car next to Gordo, shoving him over so he's sitting up, then let him lean into me when he falls over.

"No, Astrid, no," says Dad when he sees I'm planning to go with him.

"How else are you going to get there?" I ask. "It's not like we can phone an ambulance or something."

He punches the car roof a few times and then, without saying anything else, spins around and marches into the house. When he returns a couple of minutes later, I ask, "Did you tell Mom we're going?"

He nods.

"What did she say?"

He scrunches his eyebrows and doesn't answer. Instead, he opens the door and gets in behind the wheel. "We're turning around at the first sign of trouble," he says.

"Good," I say.

Dad noses the car out of the driveway and races down the street. He's driving way too fast, and when he turns left I almost fall over Gordo.

"Dad, slow down," I say. My arm's already aching from holding Gordo's head up.

Dad glances back at us, then slows the car. We drive along in silence for a while, and to avoid seeing Gordo's slack face, I look out the window.

There are so many people walking, even though it's early.

Gordo groans and shifts, and his arm falls across mine. It's so hot it feels like sunbaked clay, and I want to move my arm away, but if I do he'll fall over, so instead I blink back tears and sit still. All I can feel is the heat on my arm.

"How far now?" I ask Dad.

"Soon," he says, but that seems to jinx things, because as soon as he says it, we turn a corner and there's a crowd of people blocking the street.

I stiffen but then notice that these are regular people, not soldiers, and they seem to be laughing and talking. Dad honks the horn, but no one moves, and we're driving so slowly, we're hardly moving at all. Dad throws his arm across the seat and looks over his shoulder, intending to back the car up, but the crowd has closed in behind us.

"Shit," he says.

"What now?" I ask. I try to keep my voice even, but the heat of Gordo's arm sears into me.

Dad honks again and a few people move out of the way, but not enough to let us get anywhere. Dad turns on the car radio, but, like yesterday, there's nothing but military marches, and he turns it off again.

Someone bangs on the hood of the car, and Dad unrolls the window. I hold my breath as Dad says, "Hey, what's going on?"

The man slaps the hood again and laughs and says, "Rawlings is coming. He's taken over the government, and he's coming to talk to the people."

"Ah…" says Dad.

"Rawlings? Here?" My voice gives away how scared that thought makes me, but Dad says "Shhh" and leans out the window.

"My son's sick. I need to get to the clinic," he says.

"The way is blocked to the ring road," the man says.

I'm amazed at how Dad keeps his cool, because he says, "Thank you" before he rolls the window back up, but then it's like someone has punctured a balloon. He slumps in his seat, and his head falls back against the headrest.

"What are we going to do?!" I wail. I can't help it. Gordo's so hot, he's taking up all the oxygen in the car. The air-conditioning isn't enough to cool him down. And now Rawlings is coming. Here.

Dad takes a deep breath, then says, "Get out, Astrid. We're going to walk."

"What?" We're in the middle of the street. What about the soldiers, and Rawlings?

"Get out." Dad's voice is like iron, and I know there's no point in arguing. A deep shiver runs down my back.

Dad pulls the car close to the side of the road and we get out.

"Stay with me, Astrid. Stick close."

Dad strides quickly through the crowd, carrying Gordo like a baby, and I have to run to keep up. But he's easy to follow, and for the first time in my life I'm glad of our blond hair. At first people jostle us as we go, but Dad keeps shouting that he's trying to get to the clinic, and soon people move out of the way and a narrow path clears for us. Dad picks up his pace, and the three of us race along.

It's a long way to the clinic. We come to a group of people fighting with soldiers. Men shout, and soldiers wave guns. My throat swells in fear, and I choke. I jump right to Dad's side, but he doesn't slow down. We're so deep in the crowd, we have no choice but to continue. I swallow hard and chant in my head, *The clinic for Gordo, the clinic for Gordo*.

We race past, and the fighters take no notice of us.

When we reach the clinic at last, Dad staggers up the steps to the verandah and sinks into a chair. Sweat pours down his face.

"Do we have an appointment?" I ask as I sit down next to him.

He shakes his head.

Of course, I think. *Stupid question. How could we have an appointment when the phones aren't working?*

Dad shifts Gordo so he lies with his bum on the chair and his head in my lap. "I'll be right back," Dad says, and he disappears inside the building.

Gordo's head feels like a bomb in my lap; I hardly dare to move or even breathe. Two women with small children are also waiting on the verandah. The kids stare at me. One of the women says something to me, and I know I should understand what she says, I know I should say something back, but I can't summon the energy to do anything at all, so I close my eyes to hold back the tears, even though I know I'm being rude.

Gordo and I stay like that until a hand on my shoulder wakes me, and a smiling woman hands me a glass of water.

"Oh…" I say, confused.

"Drink up," says the woman.

I don't know what to do, but she smiles even more and says, "It's purified water. Drink it," so I take it from her and sip. It's cold and fresh and the most wonderful thing in the world. I drink the whole glass.

"Feel better?" she asks.

"Yes, thank you."

I struggle to sit straighter in the chair, and it's only then that I notice the woman is holding a cloth to Gordo's forehead.

"Do you work here?" I ask.

"I'm a nurse. Your brother's very sick, but he's going to be okay." She puts her hand on my arm and says again, "He's going to be okay," and even though I've never seen this woman before in my life, I believe her, and I breathe more easily.

"Where's my dad?" I ask.

"He's filling out some papers."

"Will the doctor see my brother soon?"

She frowns. "The doctor's on his way, but…"

"The crowds," I say, and she nods.

"What's going on out there?"

"People are celebrating."

"Celebrating?" I shake my head in confusion. How could you celebrate soldiers breaking someone out of jail and taking over the government?

"Rawlings will be our savior," the woman says.

"We saw some people fighting," I say.

"They are wrong," she says.

I should have some response to that, but I don't. Even though I know I should worry about what's going on in Ghana, I can't. Worrying about Gordo and about Mom is enough. Thinking about Mom makes me think about Piper, and then I'm even more worried, because who's taking care of her now that Mom's gone completely nuts? Saying that, even in my head, makes me shiver. Mom's gone nuts. It's true. Why else would I be here? If she were in her right mind, she would be here with Dad and I'd be safe at home, taking care of Piper. Instead, I'm sitting in a clinic halfway across town with my sick brother's head in my lap, and Mom's losing her mind at home. Life's not fair, but there's nothing I can do about it right now, so I shift Gordo's head to the softer part of my stomach and close my eyes again.

When Dad comes back, I go to the bathroom and wet the cloth for Gordo's head again. Then we sit for hours— maybe it isn't hours, but it feels like it—before a doctor comes outside and waves us into the building.

It's cool inside, but Gordo complains loudly when he's under the air conditioner, so the doctor leads him to a window, where he looks into Gordo's eyes and mouth and takes his temperature. When he's done, he perches on a stool and says, "Your son most likely has malaria." He smiles when he speaks, like it's a good thing, but Dad's face gets all blotchy and he stammers, "Malaria?"

We're silent while we take this in. Then Dad says, "Is there anything…"

"The key is to get the fever down, and to keep him hydrated," says the doctor. "I advise you to take him home. Sometimes we take malaria patients in and give them a saline drip, but to be honest, in your case I think he'll be better off at home."

He doesn't have to explain what he means. Everyone knows people get sicker when they go to the hospital. When Thema's mother went into hospital for surgery last year, her family had to bring in all her meals and boil her drinking water.

"Can you give me anything for him?"

"He's taking Chloroquine?"

Dad nods, but my stomach flips over on itself. Chloroquine is the nasty-tasting malaria medicine we have to take every week, but Gordo only *sometimes* takes his Chloroquine. Often, he leaves it in his mouth until Mom's not looking, then sticks it in his pocket to flush away later. I've seen him do it.

"Then he'll be fine. Keep his fever down and give him plenty to drink."

"Dad," I say. My voice is barely a whisper, so I say it again, louder. "Dad? Gordo doesn't always take his Chloroquine."

Both Dad and the doctor stare at me like I've grown another head, and the light changes in their eyes as they both understand what I've said.

"How often?" Dad asks, but I don't know.

"Mostly he takes it. I think." My stomach's not just flipping, it's dancing inside me now, because Dad's face goes from blotchy to bright red, and the doctor moves back over to Gordo. I take hold of Dad's hand, and we squeeze each other's fingers while the doctor looks into Gordo's eyes again.

"My advice is still the same," says the doctor when he's done.

"Because…"

"Because your son's still a healthy, well-fed boy."

After a second, Dad nods his head, gathers Gordo into his arms and says, "Come on, Astrid," and we walk out of the building.

There are fewer people on the street now, and it's easier to walk.

"I'll make sure he takes it from now on," I say. But Dad doesn't answer—he just keeps walking until he's settled Gordo into the car. Then he leans on the hood and wipes the sweat from his eyes before he opens the front door and says, "Get in, Astrid. Let's get Gordo home."

Mom rushes out of the house when we drive up. She has this look on her face like we're going to have solved everything, but that look disappears as soon as Dad opens the door and steps out of the car.

"Oh, Richard," she says.

Dad reaches into the back seat and helps Gordo out, and then, without saying a word, he picks him up and carries him into the house.

"Gordo's going to be okay, Mom," I say. But I don't think she hears me, because she's running after Dad.

SIXTEEN

No one wakes me for school, and since the power has come on and the room is cool, I sleep late. When I get up, I walk down the hall to Gordo's room. The curtains are drawn and the room is gloomy and quiet, like a room in an old people's home. The smell of sickness as I enter makes me catch my breath.

Gordo's eyes are closed, and I have to look hard at his chest to be sure he's breathing. When his chest moves, I take a deep breath of my own.

Mom is sitting on the edge of Gordo's bed. She doesn't move as I enter, but when I say, "Hi, Mom," she smiles at me.

"Is he better?" I ask.

"His fever broke last night," she says.

"So that means he's better?"

"It means…Dad thinks he's going to be okay." Mom runs her finger along Gordo's hairline, which he would never let her do if he was feeling well. Her words sound good, but they don't travel far.

Piper calls out from her room.

"Go get her, will you?" Mom says. "Get her fed and dressed too." She adds "Please" as I leave the room, though she doesn't turn around. She probably hasn't noticed that I'm not dressed for school. She probably doesn't care. I don't bother complaining that she's asking me to take care of Piper yet again. There's no point.

When Piper and I go downstairs, Dad's alone at the table. He's dressed for work but looks like he hasn't slept. His hair is a mess and the wrinkles around his eyes look deeper.

"Hi, Dad," I say.

"Hi, girls." He takes Piper from me. She snuggles into his lap and plays with her toes.

"Are you going to work?"

"Not this morning, Astrid." His voice sounds completely unlike him—thin and uncertain—and it makes my breath constrict to hear it.

"Is it Gordo?"

"Gordo's going to be fine," says Dad, but in that same thin voice.

"Dad," I say, "he doesn't look fine. Mom doesn't think he's fine."

"I know, but he is." Dad smiles. "He'll be fine, Astrid. Your mother…" He doesn't finish his sentence. After a minute, he says, "You don't mind taking care of Piper today, do you, honey?"

"What about school?" I really want to see Thema.

"School's closed."

"Can I have Thema over?"

"I don't think so. We should keep off the streets for a day or two. I think Thema's family will feel the same way."

"But Dad…" It was only yesterday that Dad and I ran through the streets taking Gordo to the clinic. Can he have forgotten that?

"I know, I know. Yesterday we had to, but today we don't, so you and Gordo and Piper will stay home today."

"Great," I say. It's like I'm grounded. Again. As if helping to get Gordo to the clinic yesterday wasn't enough.

I need a break.

I need to see Thema.

Even Thomas hasn't been around to talk to.

How come no one's thinking about what I need?

I get up to go outside, but Dad says, "I'm counting on you to be good about this, Astrid. Mom needs our support right now. You can do your bit by taking care of Piper." He picks Piper up from his lap and hands her to me.

I can never be mad at Piper, but I cross my arms, which leaves Dad holding her up to me.

"Astrid," he says. His voice is tired—but then, so am I.

"'Strid," says Piper, and my arms instinctively reach out and take her. She throws her arms around me, and I hug her close. What kind of a creep would I be to use Piper as a way to get back at Dad?

Dad stands up and pulls his car keys out of his pocket.

"Where are you going?" I ask.

Dad takes a deep breath. "There's some extra Chloroquine at the office," he says. "I won't be long."

"Can I come with you? We can bring Piper, so Mom can rest for a bit."

"No." His voice has that final tone, but I still say, "How come? How come I can't?"

"Astrid…" He stops and I think he's going to walk out the door without saying anything else, but then he turns to me and says, "Honey, yesterday people were celebrating, and yesterday we had to get Gordo to the clinic, but today there are more soldiers on the streets. And today you don't have to go out. Some of the soldiers have been breaking into houses and taking things, sometimes alcohol, so now there are drunken boys with guns on the street, and I don't want you out there."

"Breaking into houses?"

"Don't worry about that. It's not going to happen to us. We're fine here in this neighborhood." Dad smiles at me, but I'm not smiling back. Drunken soldiers on the street, and Dad's going into town? All the anger I was feeling toward him a minute ago evaporates like it never existed. The room feels small all of a sudden.

"Don't go, Dad," I say, but he shrugs and says, "I have to. Your mother will never forgive me if something happens to Gordo."

It's hot as anything outside. I push Piper in her hammock and stare at the clouds. Thomas's radio is locked in the shed, and I don't have a key. It's hot, hot, hot and I'm bored, bored, bored, but I don't want to go inside in case I run into Mom. In the end, I gather Piper onto my lap and squish into the hammock with her.

When Dad's car turns into the driveway, Piper and I leave the hammock and run toward him. He pulls up to the house but stays in the car, his head slumped over the steering wheel, and he only raises his head when Piper calls out, "Daddy." His face is white, and he looks way worse than he did when he left this morning.

"Dad, what happened?" I ask.

"How's Gordo?" he says.

"Not great. Mom's been with him all morning."

Dad shakes his head. He rubs his hand along his neck and over his face.

"What happened?" I ask.

"I'll go check on Gordo," he says, opening the door and getting out.

"Dad!" I say.

He looks at me properly for the first time. "I'm sorry, Astrid. I've got a lot on my mind."

"Dad. I'm not a little kid."

"I sometimes forget that, Astrid."

"Mom's worried sick about Gordo. She's losing her mind. She doesn't have any time for me at all, and now you won't even talk to me." I don't plan to say all those things. They just come out.

Dad puts his car keys in his pocket and reaches for me and Piper. "It's been hard for you, hasn't it, Astrid?"

"Yes," I say.

Our hug is the longest, strongest one we've had for a long time. We say all kinds of things to each other through that hug, like how sorry we are and how we each need the other to be strong. At last Dad lets me go and says, "You're the best, Astrid. Truly."

Those words wipe away days and days of frustration, and I smile at him.

"But Mom…" I say.

Dad takes my head in his hands and bends down so we're eye to eye. "She'll be fine, Astrid. Once Gordo is better and she gets some rest, she'll be fine. We all react to stress differently, and she's taken all of this very hard. She feels responsible for both of you, and she's angry at herself for bringing you here. This coup and Gordo getting sick have made a bad situation for her even worse."

I nod. I wish he'd told me that before. It helps me understand some of the things she's flipped out about over the past couple of months.

"She's acting kind of crazy," I say, but I laugh a little when I say it.

"I'll go and check on her," Dad says.

"But Dad, what happened?"

I don't think he knows his hands are shaking.

"I was stopped at a roadblock. A soldier…" He pauses and closes his eyes. When he opens them, he says, "I'm fine, Astrid. I'm shaken, that's all. He didn't hurt me. I shouldn't have told you."

"Dad, I'm glad you're okay," I say.

"It'll be over soon. Rawlings and his men will settle into being the new government. They'll sort things out," says Dad. "Until then, we'll be fine." He takes a deep breath and slowly exhales. "I'll go see your mom and Gordo. And Astrid—thank you."

SEVENTEEN

A few days later, Dad drives me and Piper over to Thema's house.

"Are you sure we should?" I ask.

"If we stick to the backroads, we'll be okay."

Life seems to be getting back to normal. Thomas and Abena are back at work. The egg lady came by yesterday. Two of Gordo's street friends poked their heads around the gate, looking for him.

Gordo's much better. He sits up in bed and eats a bit of food when Abena makes his favorite things, like grilled cheese sandwiches. Mom still spends all her time with him, and I'm not sure if Dad arranged for me and Piper to go to Thema's house for Mom's sake or for mine, but either way, I'm happy to be away from Mom's dreary face and the stale air in Gordo's room.

Thema and I swim in the pool until we're waterlogged, then we have a snack, and then Thema's mom tells her she has to finish folding the laundry, so Piper and I head out back to where Piper's hammock is still slung between two trees. When we get there, Ebo's already lying in it.

"You're still here, I see," he says.

"We're staying until lunchtime," I say.

"I mean, you're still in Ghana. You didn't leave."

I'm confused, but then I remember the conversation we had after Rawlings first attempted a coup, and how I said that if it got dangerous we could all leave.

"No…" Once again, I don't know what to say. I'd like to say something, but before I can figure out what, Ebo says, "Piper, come sit with me," and he pulls her up onto the hammock with him.

I push the hammock so they swing gently back and forth.

"Did you want to leave?" Ebo asks.

"No," I say before I can think about it, but it's true. I haven't wanted to leave, not even once. "I'd like to go back to school, though," I add.

Ebo laughs. "Back to Sister Mary?"

"Was she your teacher too?"

"Two years ago. She had tarantulas that year."

I shudder. Snakes I can handle, but tarantulas would be a different thing.

"Does she still make you memorize poems?"

"Yes."

"And dissect rats?"

"Yeah."

"She's cool," says Ebo, and I have to admit, she is.

Thema comes out and we spend the rest of the morning playing badminton and lying in the hammock.

At home, I go upstairs to say hi to Gordo while Mom puts Piper down for her nap, but he's asleep, so I tiptoe out of his room.

"It's going to take him a long time to recover completely," says Mom when we meet in the hallway.

I think it's going to take her a long time too. Her eyes still have dark shadows under them, but there's a bit of a smile in them, which I haven't seen for a while.

When lunch is ready, Mom and I sit at the table together. We don't say much, and it seems strange it being just the two of us. To fill the silence, I tell her about swimming at Thema's house and about a new song Thema's learning. She listens with a smile, so I keep talking.

When the banging on the door starts, I drop my sandwich in my lap.

"Don't answer it," Mom says.

The banging comes again.

"Shhh," whispers Mom. Neither of us moves, and I can tell from the wideness of Mom's eyes that she's thinking the same thing I am.

What if it's a soldier at the door?

I clench my jaw so hard it hurts. Neither of us speaks or even breathes. Then there's a noise at the back of the house.

Through the window, I see a soldier pointing a gun at Thomas, who has frozen, bent over with his shovel in his hand.

Mom rises out of her chair. "Oh…" she says.

Thomas and the soldier turn. When the soldier sees us, he shouts something I don't understand. Thomas drops his shovel and shakes his head. The soldier shouts again, and Mom goes to the window.

The soldier jabs his gun at Thomas.

No one breathes.

Then Mom raises her hand. "I'll open the door," she shouts. The soldier marches Thomas around the house.

Mom and I rush to the front door.

"Go into the kitchen and lock the door," she says to me, but I don't move. "Go," she says.

I can't.

I can't leave her here with the soldier on the other side of the door.

I take her hand. "Ready," I say.

Mom opens her mouth to say something, but I hold her hand tighter.

She draws in a deep breath and opens the door.

The soldier stares at us. He lets his eyes wander from our feet to our faces. He says something we don't understand.

Mom starts shaking. A tingling sensation runs up my fingers, into my arms and through my whole body, but the two of us stand together. Neither of us moves. The soldier speaks again, and this time Thomas says, "He asks where you are from."

"Canada," says Mom.

The soldier speaks again, and Thomas says, "He wants to know how long you've been living here."

"Five months," says Mom.

The soldier gestures to Mom's purse, hanging near the door. He uses his gun, so it swings toward our faces, and both of us gasp. The solider laughs and points at the purse again. Mom takes it off the hook and gives it to him. He slings it on his shoulder and then, without saying anything, he turns and walks away. We watch until he leaves the driveway and turns down the road.

Mom sags against the door. I let go of her hand and lean on the other side. Thomas sinks to the floor at our feet. None of us moves or says anything. My heart is beating so fast I feel my blood rushing past my ears. The three of us stay there, silent.

When I go to bed, Dad comes into my room. He sits on the edge of my bed and says, "You were brave today."

"I wish you'd been here," I say.

"So do I." His voice sounds tired, worn out.

"Why do you think he left?" I ask. I've been thinking about it all day. He could easily have barged into the house and taken anything he wanted. Mom and Thomas and I wouldn't have stopped him. Not with that gun.

"Was it because we're foreigners?" I ask.

Dad shakes his head. "I don't know, but I'd say yes, probably," he says.

There's nothing more to say after that, so he leaves and I lie in bed thinking about how Ebo said his dad would never leave Ghana and about how easily we could.

EIGHTEEN

"Joanne, go to bed," says Dad a couple of mornings later.

"I think I'll sit with Gordo a bit," Mom says, but Dad says, "Joanne. Please. Look at yourself."

She doesn't move, but when Gordo says, "Astrid's going to read to me," she lets Dad lead her out of the room.

"Read to you?" I ask. Gordo's a lot better, but he's still weak and not allowed to leave his bedroom.

Gordo frowns. "I had to say something. She doesn't want me to be left alone. She's afraid I'll get sick again. She's afraid I'm going to die."

I sit on the edge of the bed. For a little kid, Gordo can be really perceptive sometimes.

"Plus, she smells," he adds.

That sounds funny, but neither of us laughs, because it's true. She hasn't had a bath or changed her clothes since Gordo got sick. We're both silent for a minute.

Dad comes back in and says, "Mom's taking a nap. Abena's agreed to keep an eye on Piper, and I'm going to work. I won't be long, but I want you to let Mom sleep. If Abena needs anything—help with Piper or anything else—I'm counting on you to help her out. Gordo, that means you too."

"You're going to work?" I say.

"I'll be fine."

It's not him I'm worried about. This will be the first time he's left the house since the soldier came. I must look anxious, because he says, "Thomas says the soldiers are under control now, so we don't have to worry."

"Soldiers?" says Gordo.

Dad sighs, but he sits on the end of Gordo's bed and tells him what's happened. I expect Gordo to be all mad about missing the soldiers, but instead his face turns pale, and his mouth sets in a grimace.

Dad kisses his forehead and says, "It's over now, Gordo. Don't worry." To me he says, "I won't be long," and he leaves the room.

Gordo throws back the sheet and swings his legs to the side of the bed.

"What are you doing?" I ask.

"Going to see Kwame and Yafeo," he says.

"You're not allowed," I say. Like not being allowed to do something has ever stopped him before. "Gordo, I'm serious."

"So am I." He pulls on shorts and a T-shirt and shoves his feet into his sandals.

"You're still sick, Gordo."

He turns his face to me. "I want to see them," he says.

"The soldiers?"

"No. Kwame and Yafeo."

"Get back into bed."

"No."

"Gordo, I'm telling Mom unless you take off your shoes and get back into bed right now."

Even that threat might not have stopped him, but he must suddenly feel tired, because he reaches his hand out to the bed, then sinks onto it.

"You go, Astrid," he says.

"As if," I say.

"Please."

"How come you want to see them so much?" I ask.

"Please. I just do."

"That's not a good answer, Gordo," I say, and I'm about to leave the room when he says, "I want to make sure they're okay."

His face looks feverish again. "Please," he whines. Usually that whiny voice drives me nuts, but today it scares me.

"Please, Astrid, please?" His face goes all blotchy. He's crying for real now, and it makes him gulp.

"Gordo, shut up—you'll wake up Mom."

That doesn't stop him. If anything, it makes him worse. He's snotty and gulping and generally getting really upset over a couple of street kids. If he has this much energy, he can go find them himself.

"Fine. Go yourself," I say.

Gordo takes in a deep breath and wipes his nose on his arm. I follow as he makes his way down the stairs and across the hallway to the front door. I know I shouldn't let him go. When he reaches the front door, he leans against it for a second, and I say, "Go sit outside, Gordo. I'll go."

He doesn't put up a fight.

Gordo tells me how to find Kwame and Yafeo. I turn left at the end of the driveway and walk two blocks down the street, across an empty lot to another street, then along that street to a hut on the corner.

I stand in the road and call, "Ko ko ko."

A woman steps out of the hut. She eyes me up and down but doesn't say anything.

"I'm Gordo's sister," I say. I don't know if she speaks English, although most people around here do.

Two boys poke their heads around the side of the hut, and I recognize them as two of the boys that come to our house.

"Is Gordo better?" one of them asks.

"He's had malaria."

The three of them nod. Everyone knows about malaria.

"But he's better now?" The boy's face is pinched with concern, and when I nod, his whole face changes with his smile.

The woman goes into the hut and comes back out again with a plastic glass of water, which she hands to me. I take a sip even though Mom would have a thousand fits if she knew, because it seems rude not to have at least some of it.

"Gordo asked me to get you," I say to the boys, and they don't wait for any more invitation before they hop across the ditch and run onto the road. I hand the glass back to the woman and say thank you in Twi, then follow them.

When we reach the house, we go around to the back to see if Gordo's there. He is, and so are Abena and Piper and Thomas. They are all sitting under the tree, drinking lemonade.

"Kwame and Yafeo are here," I say to Gordo. He grins, and the boys run up to him. They jabber away in Twi—so fast, it's hard to distinguish words—but Gordo listens, and he must understand them because he laughs at the same time Abena and Thomas do.

"What are they saying?" I ask Thomas.

"They're telling about when a soldier came and took stuff from their mama's stall."

"Why is it funny?" I ask.

"They make it sound funny. What else are they going to do?"

Kwame or Yafeo sits down next to Abena and holds his arms out for Piper. I'm about to give him my ice-queen stare and say "No, we don't let street people and strangers touch her," but I shut my mouth, because she crawls into his lap like she's done it a dozen times before.

Gordo's face is still pale, but he laughs at the boys' jokes and talks easily with them. His feverish look has gone, and I suddenly understand that he was really worried about them. To him, they are more than just boys who live in the neighborhood and sneak up the drive to hang out at our house. They are his friends.

Piper plays happily with the boys, and my face burns with embarrassment. I've never even learned which boy is Kwame and which is Yafeo, so when Gordo talks, I listen, so that in future I will know.

NINETEEN

School opens again. It's been two weeks since the coup, and now it's so close to the end of term that I wonder why they bothered bringing us all back. When Dad tells us we're going to school in the morning, I wait for Mom to freak out and say no way, but she doesn't. The only thing she says is, "I'd better make sure you have clean uniforms," and she gets up from the table to go check. She's looking better. The bags under her eyes have gone, she doesn't smell bad, and she's washed and combed her hair. She even put on a pretty sundress this morning.

Gordo shrugs, and I decide it's best not to say anything.

It's great to see everyone, and even Bassam doesn't bother me when he comes into the classroom. It's strange. He walks in with his head hanging and sits behind me.

I pull my hair around my shoulder so he can't reach it, but he doesn't even try. Thema and I frown at each other.

"What's wrong with him?" I whisper to her.

She shrugs, and then we both sit straight as Sister Mary walks into the room. She has the snake in her pocket. She must have come to school when it was closed to pick it up.

"Who wants to feed the snake?" she asks as she lowers it into the terrarium. All the boys' hands go up, but Bassam doesn't seem as enthusiastic as usual. Normally, he bounces out of his seat to get her attention. Today, he raises his hand slowly. Sister Mary chooses Peter, so Bassam lowers his hand and slumps back in his desk. He doesn't grumble as he usually does when someone else gets picked. I wonder what's going on.

The morning goes slowly. Sister Mary sets us a bunch of math questions to work on silently, but she has to send three people onto the breezeway for talking out of turn (not me, thank goodness), and no matter how many times she tells us to be quiet, the room always has a buzz in it. Finally break comes, and we all surge out of doors.

"What's up with Bassam?" Thema asks Harpreet as we run to the tamarind tree.

"Didn't you hear?"

"Hear what?"

"Bassam's house was raided," says Harpreet. As she speaks, her eyes glitter in a way that makes me shudder a bit.

"You mean by soldiers?" asks Thema.

Harpreet leans in close and whispers, "They've taken his dad to jail because he's a hoarder."

I don't know what to say to this. Bassam's dad in jail? The image of the soldier pointing a gun at Thomas fills my eyes, and for a moment I can't breathe.

"A hoarder?" Thema asks.

"That's why there's nothing in the stores," Harpreet says.

"Nothing in the stores because Bassam's dad hoards it all?" Thema asks.

"No, stupid, because lots of people do it. That's called corruption, and that's what Rawlings is getting rid of." Harpreet sounds so sure, but Thema doesn't look convinced.

"Poor Bassam," says Thema.

"So I guess his party's canceled," says Harpreet.

I don't like her much, I decide.

When I get home after school, I find Thomas in the back garden, listening to the radio and raking.

"Don't you get tired of listening to that?" I ask.

"Astrid, the future of our country is in that radio," he says.

"What do you mean?"

"Whatever Rawlings says to the country, that's our future."

I think about that for a minute before saying, "My dad says Rawlings doesn't know what he's doing."

"Hmmm…well," says Thomas, as if he's thinking about what he's going to say. "It's not going to be easy, that's for sure." He doesn't look at me when he says that, as if he's hiding something.

"I thought you were happy Rawlings is in power now," I say.

"I was. I am. I think I am," he says.

I'm confused. At first Thomas couldn't stop talking about how excited he was. But then the soldier came. Maybe that's what's wrong. Even though Gordo's better and Thomas says the soldiers aren't breaking into people's houses anymore, I know all of us are still jumpy.

"But there are also some hard things about it," I say, to show I understand.

Thomas lifts his rake and tips it on end so he can pull off a leaf that's stuck in the tines. He says, "You're a smart girl, Asteroid."

I'm happy he calls me Asteroid, because that shows he's in a better mood, but he ruins it with a frown that creases his whole face.

"Is there something else?" I ask.

"Some soldiers went to the market. They harassed Esi." He doesn't look at me when he says it.

"What!"

"She doesn't want to go back because she's afraid they'll come again."

"I don't understand. Why would they?" I ask.

"They've beaten up some women in the market. They call them hoarders." His face is so sad, I don't know what to say. This can't be right. It was hard enough to think about Bassam's dad being a hoarder, and his family is rich. I know for sure that Thomas and Esi aren't rich. How can anyone think Esi's a hoarder?

"Does that mean you can't sell your animals anymore?" I ask.

He nods. "Not for now anyway."

"So you can't buy your house?"

"Not right now." His voice quavers, and he leans into his raking. "I shouldn't have told you that, Astrid," he says.

I blush. I hate feeling helpless.

"Will you do me a favor? Can you ask Abena to bring me my tea?" Thomas asks.

"Sure," I say. At least it's something I can do.

TWENTY

It's raining on our last day at school. At home in Canada, I'm used to rain that soaks in slowly. Here, we're drenched in seconds, and the cars and buses make waves in the street as they pass. The dusty school grounds have already turned to mud, so we have no choice but to run into the breezeway for cover.

Some boys kick a soccer ball around on the tiles, and a bunch of kids dangle their legs over the rails. Thema stands near the classroom door with Harpreet. Her face looks plastic, like she's listening to Harpreet but not interested. When she catches my eye, she says something to Harpreet and walks over to me. She puts her hand on her hip, flips some non-existent long hair over her shoulder and says, "You'll never guess what I've heard."

Her imitation of Harpreet is so good, I splutter with laughter.

"What did she hear?" I ask.

Thema laughs. "Who knows? I left before she could tell me."

Sister Mary marches down the breezeway, scattering kids as she comes. When she gets to the classroom door, she says, "Well, go on, in you go," and we all crowd inside.

Summer holidays start tomorrow, and it's hard to pay attention. Sister Mary doesn't even try to make us work. Instead, we clean the classroom. We have to collect all our papers into bundles to take home and gather pens and pencils into a box for next year's kids.

By the time the bell rings at the end of the day, our classroom looks completely different. There's nothing on the walls except for the rolled-up maps, and our desks have been scrubbed and all the stickers peeled off. We each have a neat pile of papers to take home. Even the snake cage is empty, and the snake is safe in Sister Mary's pocket.

"Goodbye, Sister Mary," we chant before she lets us out of the room.

"Have a good summer, everyone," she says.

Thema and I saunter to the parking lot. "I think I'm going to miss her," Thema says.

"Sister Mary?"

"Yeah."

I only think about it for a second before I say, "Me too."

After lunch, Gordo and I sit outside under the tree. I read, and Gordo watches a spider spin a web. I noticed it first and almost swatted it away, but Gordo puffed out his chest like a rooster and said, "It's a brown button spider," as if that meant I'd be a criminal to touch it, so I plunked down into the chair and picked up my book instead. As long as the spider stays over there on the branch, Gordo can watch it as long as he wants.

Watership Down is boring. I hate to say it, but it is. With a sigh, I put it aside and watch Gordo studying the spider instead. For a boy who's usually running, he can be really still when there's some kind of creature around.

Thomas comes around the side of the house. He has a frown on his face, and he stares at Gordo like he's trying to decide whether to say something.

"Thomas?" I say.

"What are you doing?" he asks Gordo.

Gordo points to the spider.

Thomas takes a deep breath and says, "Gordo, I need some help. Come help me."

"Awww," says Gordo. "Can't you ask Astrid instead?"

"I need your help," says Thomas, and his voice is sharp, like I've never heard it before. He jabs the shovel into the ground by his foot. "I've found some snake eggs that need to be moved. Come on, it will only take a minute."

"I'll watch the spider," I say, though watching spiders is about as exciting as watching paint dry, and I shove Gordo out of the way and stand under the branch to get a clear view. Gordo runs over to Thomas and says, "What kind of snake? Can I keep one?" as they disappear around the corner.

Something is wrong with Thomas. In the past few days he hasn't sung or listened to the radio or whittled. He says hello as usual, but there's something different about the way he talks on the rare occasions he says anything. I keep asking if he's okay, and he keeps saying he is, but I don't believe him. He seems preoccupied, and I guess he's been thinking about his animals and the house that he can't buy.

I stand under the spider while it does nothing until Gordo comes back. I don't know why the spider has to be watched, but I've given up trying to understand Gordo and his creatures.

"What kind of snake was it?" I ask.

"Python. I couldn't keep any of the eggs," says Gordo absently. He's already totally focused on the spider, and I might as well not be here.

I find Thomas sitting near the laundry area, drinking tea. His whittling knife lies across his leg, and he holds a broken bird in his hand. I've seen him make dozens of animals, and I've never seen him break one.

"What happened?" I ask, sliding down next to him.

He gathers the bird pieces and folds them into his hand.

"Have you finished your book?" he asks.

"I didn't like it," I say.

"What was it about?"

He's trying to get to me talk about my book so I won't ask him any questions, but there's something wrong, I know it, so I pick up a piece of wood on which he's drawn the outline of an elephant and say, "What happened to the bird?"

He opens his hand. The bird is still beautiful, even though one of its wings is broken.

"It snapped. It happens," he says.

"Why? Why did it snap?"

"It just did," he says.

I pick the bird and its wing out of his hand and hold the two pieces together. "Can you fix it?" I ask.

He takes a long drink of his tea and puts the cup on the ledge, then stands up and wipes the grass from his pants.

"I don't think so, Astrid," he says.

He picks up his shovel and walks away, and I'm left holding a beautiful, broken bird in my hand. I'll take it inside and glue it back together. It can be fixed. I'll show him.

TWENTY-ONE

I hear Thomas and Dad talking in the driveway on Monday morning, so I already know what Thomas is going to say when he comes to find me. I see him coming, so I pick up my book and walk toward the door.

"Asteroid," he calls, but I pretend I don't hear and keep walking until I'm in the kitchen.

He won't follow me in here.

Abena is here, though, and she says, "Thomas is looking for you. He wants to tell you something."

"Stupid Thomas," I say, but not loud enough for her to hear.

"You go find him," she says. I want to pretend I can't hear her either, but since she's standing a couple of feet away from me, I can't. She opens the door.

"Go on," she says.

Thomas is across the yard, raking, so I walk toward the back, where Gordo is watching the spider spin its web again. Gordo takes no notice when I get there, so I sit next to him and watch too. The spider moves slowly and hardly seems to be doing anything, but then she reaches the other side of the web, and suddenly a new line connects the two pieces together.

Thomas comes across the yard, so I stand up to go somewhere else, but he catches my eye and I sit back down again.

"Go away," I say to Gordo.

"Get lost," says Gordo.

"Go on." I don't want to have this conversation with Gordo here, even though he'll have to find out soon.

"Hi, you two," says Thomas.

"She's almost done," Gordo says, pointing at the web. Thomas nods, then says, "Astrid, can you help me for a minute?" I nod but don't say anything as he leads me around to the front of the house.

"Astrid, I'm leaving. I have to go."

"Fine," I say. My voice is higher than I intend.

"Esi wants me to say goodbye to you from her. She gave me this to give to you." He holds out a tape. The word *Blondie* is written on the case.

"Fine," I say again.

"Don't be like that, Astrid."

I glare at him. I want to speak, but my mouth won't open. Words crowd into my head but refuse to leave my mouth.

"We have to go—you know we do. Esi's afraid to go back to the market. There's nothing for her to do here. There's no future for us."

I nod, still unable to speak, and take the tape from him.

I stare at my feet.

"We'll talk again before I go," he says.

I make myself get up early the next morning and go outside to wait for Thomas. It's so early the roosters are still crowing, but I want to make sure I'm there when Thomas comes. I sit on the step and lean against the house.

The wheelbarrow man walks past, then another man with a bundle of wood on his head, then three women carrying plastic tubs, and then, finally, Thomas. He turns into the drive and smiles at me as always.

"Asteroid," he says.

"Hi, Thomas."

Instead of going to the shed as usual, he comes and sits next to me. He pulls off his toque and jacket and plunks them in a heap between us.

"I'm sorry for yesterday," I say.

"It's okay, Astrid. I understand."

"And I'm sorry you and Esi have to go."

He takes a deep breath. "Me too."

I finger the bundle on my lap.

"You understand why we have to go, don't you?" Thomas asks.

"Not really, but I guess it's because of what happened at the market. And the soldier who came here."

"It's not safe there for Esi. I don't want her there."

"Yeah," I say.

"And she doesn't want to go back there either."

"Yeah." I understand that. I can't even imagine what it was like.

"But Thomas, I was thinking: What if I sell your animals at school for you when the summer holidays are over? I bet loads of people would buy them."

Thomas leans back against the wall and closes his eyes, and I think I've said something bad. Something insulting. But then he opens his eyes and pulls me into a hug. "You have such a good heart, Astrid."

"So it's a good idea, right?" I ask.

"No. It's a generous idea, but not a good one."

"How come?"

"Your teachers would never let you, and neither would your parents."

I hadn't thought of that. He's right though. I can picture the look on the headmistress's face. If it weren't so sad, it would make me laugh.

"Where will you go?" I ask.

"Esi's family lives in Kumasi. We'll go there for a while."

"And you'll work with her brothers."

"Yes."

"But it won't be as good as working here," I say.

Thomas laughs. "I like Esi's brothers, and I'll be able to make more animals and sell them in their store."

"But there won't be Gordo and Piper and me."

"No, Astrid, there won't." Thomas smiles and gathers his toque and jacket. "I'd better get to work."

"Here," I say. I hand him the bundle I've been holding in my lap.

"What is it?"

"Open it and see."

Thomas peels back the paper. "Oh, Astrid," he says. He picks the bird up and cradles it in his hand. The two wings soar away from the body like the bird is in mid-flight.

"Mom helped me glue it back together," I say.

He holds it out and turns it around and around, peering at each wing.

"I can hardly see where it broke. Thank you, Astrid."

"You're welcome."

He walks away, still holding the bird up to the light.

TWENTY-TWO

On the weekend, we go to the beach. It's been over a month since we were last there. No wonder Gordo and I are excited. Dad packs a huge picnic, and Piper struts around with her swimming wings on. It takes Dad absolutely ages to convince her that she can't wear them in the car. Even Mom shows up at the car when it's time to leave.

When we get to the beach, Thema and Ebo are already there, and the four of us race into the waves. Ebo wins, so he gets to splash the rest of us, but we don't care, because the water is so refreshing.

"I could stay here all day," I say to Thema.

"Me too," she says.

Thema and I get the air mattresses from the car trunk and blow them up. I glance over at Mom, but she's paying attention to Piper. Thema and I launch ourselves and float out from the shore. The waves rock us, and I lie on my stomach and trail my fingers in the water. It's so relaxing.

When Mom calls us in for lunch I can hardly move, I'm so sleepy. Ebo is nearby, so Thema calls out to him, "Ebo, come pull us into shore."

He ducks underwater and disappears until he surfaces behind us.

"Why would I want to do that?" he asks.

"Because Astrid's sleepy," Thema says.

I blush, as usual, and turn away from Ebo, but he swims to my air mattress and tickles my toes until I squirm.

"Still tired?" he asks.

I laugh but say, "Yes." And I am. I feel like I need to sleep for a week. I guess I must sound convincing, because he says, "Okay," and he swims around to the front of the air mattresses and pulls us to shore.

"There you go," he says as we reach the sand.

"Thanks, Ebo," I say.

"Astrid, are you okay?" he asks.

"What do you mean?"

"I mean, after Gordo was sick and all, and your mom…and I heard a soldier came to your house."

"Yeah, but it's okay. I'm fine." It's true too. Everyone seems better—even Mom seems more normal. Not totally normal, but better. It's like her worst fears came true when Gordo got sick and the soldier came to our house, but now they're over, and she's going to be okay.

"Hmmm," he says, but he picks up a towel from the pile on the sand and wipes his face and hair, then runs up the beach to where our parents have already started eating.

Thema takes my hand and says, "Come on, Astrid, I'm starving," so the two of us rest our air mattresses against a coconut palm and join the picnic.

When we're finished eating, Ebo says, "Let's try out the boogie boards."

Gordo jumps up, spraying sand everywhere, and says, "Okay."

I don't bother getting excited, because there's no way that we're going to be allowed, but Dad says, "I'd like to try them too."

Gordo hops up and down and poses like a surfer. He swaggers around the picnic blankets and calls everyone "dude" until we're all laughing. Mr. Ampofo hands Ebo the car keys, and he and Gordo take six bodyboards out of the trunk.

"They're not full-sized surfboards, Gordo," says Mr. Ampofo. "They're for bodyboarding, not surfing."

"I know," says Gordo, and he doesn't sound disappointed at all.

"Who wants to try?" asks Mr. Ampofo.

"Me," says Ebo.

"Me," says Gordo.

"Me," says Thema.

"Me," I say.

"Me," says Dad.

I wait for Mom to say something. She stiffens, and I think, *Here we go*, but Dad takes her aside and talks to her for a minute, and when he comes back, he says, "Let's go."

If Mom is going to let us go, we're going. We each take a board and walk down the beach a bit to where there is more surf, then wade out chest deep.

Ebo and his Dad have done it before, so they go first. They point their boards toward shore and wait until a wave rises up behind them, then launch their chests across the boards and kick furiously until the wave catches them and carries them to shore. Ebo whoops as he goes.

Gordo and Thema and I try for the next wave. I can feel it building behind me, so I wait until it lifts my feet, then kick like mad. There's froth around my shoulders, and the board leaps forward, slides down the front of the wave and races to shore.

"Wow!" I say to Ebo when I get there. He grins at me and runs back out to the waves.

I do it again.

And again.

Each time, I feel like I'm flying.

The boards are better on bigger waves, but finally one comes that's so big it tips me right off my board, and I go under. Water churns around me, and something hits me on the head. For a second I rise to the surface and gulp air, but then I'm pulled under again and dragged along the bottom. Coral scrapes across my arm. Salt gets into my eyes and mouth, and when I finally reach shore and the wave recedes, I gasp and splutter. My eyes sting. My arm smarts.

My board rears up behind me as another wave comes in, and it smacks into my legs, knocking me over again. Sand piles into my bathing suit as I'm dragged back into the water. I struggle to stand, and when I do, I grab my board and wade to shore.

Gordo and Thema are already there. "Are you okay?" Thema asks.

I nod, though my eyes are still blurry. "I think I'm done," I say.

"Me too," says Thema.

"I'm going back out," says Gordo and runs out to where Ebo and Dad wait for the next wave.

I wave to Dad and point toward the cars. He waves, and Thema and I walk back to where our moms are.

When Mom sees us, she leaps to her feet. "Astrid, what happened?"

"It's nothing," I say, and I put my arm behind my back where she can't see it. But Mom has eagle eyes, and she pulls my arm toward her.

"I fell off my board," I say. My arm is sore where the scrape is.

"What is your father thinking, letting you all out there?" she says. I expect her to march down the beach and haul Dad and Gordo back, but instead she takes a deep breath.

"It's okay," she says. I think she's saying it to herself more than to me, but I smile and nod and pretend my arm isn't stinging like heck.

"Go put the board in the Ampofos' car, then come back and I'll put something on that scrape," says Mom.

"It's fine, Mom," I say, but she glares at me, and I figure I'd better not push her too far.

Thema and I put our boards in the trunk, and then I go back to where Mom's sitting. She takes my arm and peers at the scrape.

"Mom," I say, "thanks for not going berserk over this."

She lets go of my arm. "Going berserk? Is that what you think I was doing?"

"Well…" I don't want to say *yes, you were really crazy*, so instead I don't say anything.

Mom rummages around in the huge first-aid kit she always brings, and I think she's going to let my comment pass, but then she says, "You know, Astrid, I did learn something in the last few days."

"What's that?"

"When Gordo was sick, you spent your whole time taking care of Piper, and I didn't worry about either of you. Then when the soldier came, you were so strong. You helped Dad get Gordo to the clinic. You never complained. So what I learned is that you are a caring and responsible girl, and I need to respect that."

Tears explode in my eyes and pour down my face. It's all I can do to say, "Thanks, Mom."

"That doesn't mean you're allowed to run around and do whatever you want," Mom says.

"I know." I nod and laugh and cry.

"And, you know, Astrid, it is dangerous here. There are lots of things that happen here that we never had to deal with at home."

"Like malaria," I say.

"And biting ants."

"And soldiers."

"Soldiers. Yes. Things are still unsettled here. We need to look out for each other," she says.

"I know." I pause, and she opens a tube of cream and rubs something onto the scrape on my arm. I yank my arm back at the sting, but she takes it back and says, "Coral scrapes fester easily" and keeps rubbing, so I clench my teeth and let her do it. When she's done, I say, "Mom, are we going to leave?"

"We're here for the day, honey. I don't think a little scrape means we should leave, but you should probably stay out of the water."

"I mean, are we going to leave Ghana?"

She screws the lid back onto the tube of cream before she answers. "Not yet," she says.

Thema and her mom join us, and her mom says, "Would you two girls do me a favor? If I give you some money, can you two go buy some sun-spots in the village?"

"Sure," says Thema. Piper stands up and reaches out for me to pick her up.

"Can we take Piper, Mom? I promise I'll be extra careful."

Mom frowns, but then Mrs. Ampofo says, "Joanne, you and I could sneak in for a little swim if the girls take Piper."

Mom twists a strand of her hair, but then smiles and says, "Okay, yes. As long as you are extra careful with her, and don't let anyone touch her, or—"

I cut her off. "I know, Mom. I will be super extra careful."

"Okay." She gives me a small bundle of cedis. I take Piper by the hand, and she and Thema and I head toward the village.

"Your mom seems a lot better," says Thema.

"Yeah. She is."

"I'm sorry about Thomas leaving," she says.

"Me too."

We walk in silence for a while, and then Thema sings a highlife song I don't know, and I pick Piper up and we dance along with Thema as we make our way down the beach. I glance back at Mom; she's laughing with Mrs. Ampofo. Dad and Gordo are still playing on their bodyboards. Piper sings along with Thema.

It's hard to believe, after everything we've been through, but everyone seems happy today.

Including me.

HISTORICAL NOTE

None of the people in this story are real except for Jerry Rawlings. Amazing as it may seem, he really did attempt a coup, go to jail, get sentenced, then get released by some of his comrades and lead another coup. That time he was successful. Here's what happened.

On May 15, 1979, less than five weeks before elections were to be held in Ghana, Flight Lieutenant Jerry Rawlings and some other junior military officers tried to take over the government of Ghana. They were not successful, and Rawlings was put in jail. A few days later, he was tried, and he gave a speech at his trial that was broadcast over the radio to the whole country. Many people who listened to that speech were inspired by Rawlings because he talked about ending the corruption that was rampant in the government and the country.

Rawlings was sentenced to be executed, and most people thought that was the end. But on June 4, 1979, some of Rawlings's friends in the army broke into the jail and released him, because they had heard his speech and thought he could help them end the corruption they saw around them. Together, they staged a coup. They started by taking over Broadcast House, where the national radio station was, and then took over other government buildings until they were in control. Within several hours, there was a new government.

Over the next weeks, there were a lot of soldiers in the streets, some of whom were violent toward civilians, and many of the women working in the markets were harassed or even beaten because they were accused of "hoarding" goods. Many of the wealthy businessmen were sent to jail, also because they were thought to be hoarders. This was a difficult time for Ghanaians.

Rawlings ruled Ghana (with only a few short breaks) until 2001. When I was doing research for this book, I found that many Ghanaians were happy with Rawlings as a ruler, but just about as many were not. Today, Ghana has a democratically elected leader.

ACKNOWLEDGMENTS

A book like this cannot be completed without help from other people who remember more (and more accurately) than I do. First, I'd like to thank my mum for never, ever being like the mother in this story (even when she learned of the snake's nest in the garden). My dad remained calm under stress and always answered my questions, and my brother, Bruce, always knew how to have fun. Their combined memories helped me shape this book.

The unflagging support of the Wildwood writers, most particularly Laurie Elmquist, who is unflinching in telling me the truth about my writing, is most certainly the reason I'm still a writer today. I shudder to think what this book would have looked like without the guidance of Sarah Harvey, my editor at Orca. And lastly, for their ability to love me even when I'm deep in a story, I thank my husband, Michael Pardy, and my son, Rowan Jones-Pardy. Where would I be in life without the two of you?

KARI JONES spent her youth traveling around the world. She was fortunate enough to spend some years in Ghana when she was in her early teens. Kari now lives and writes in Victoria, British Columbia. For more information, visit www.karijones.ca.